About the Author

Elena Kaufman is a writer, actor and teacher from Vancouver, Canada and now living in Hamburg, Germany. She has an MSt in Creative Writing (University of Oxford) and an MA in Drama (University of Toronto). In 2002 she left Toronto and co-founded Paris Playwrights at the Shakespeare and Company bookstore, culminating in a short play festival. In 2005, she and her physicist husband relocated to Hamburg, where she acted and ran R3, a play-reading series at The Rover Rep Theatre. Her monologues appear in Smith and Kraus and Heinemann Press collections, and her one-acts were produced at festivals (FemFest in Winnipeg, FEATS Festival in Stockholm, and UBC Centennial, Vancouver). Eight of the stories in *Love Bites* are published in literary journals, and Elena is working on a mystery novel, *The Smoking Dog*. She writes from the Writers' Room, Hamburg. See elenakaufman.com; @elenadkaufman; www.facebook.com/kaufmanwrites.

D1387054

Praise for *Love Bites*

'The stories in *Love Bites* are both delicate and tough. They contain vivid, every-sense descriptions of place, as well as intriguing and affecting characters who tend to be not quite lost, but searching. Endings are unexpected – decisions get made often enough simply by default and futures are distinctly inconclusive. There's everything – grief, dependence, dementia, goodness – and smartly, it's goodness of a slightly ambiguous sort.'

Joan Barfoot, *award-winning author of 11 novels, including* Critical Injuries, *longlisted for the Man Booker Prize*

'An austere clear-sightedness characterizes these delicate portraits of missed opportunities and disconnections. Kaufman's gracefully accumulated detail creates a world – or worlds – at once disconcertingly off-beat yet wholly believable. An impressive debut.'

Dr Clare Morgan, *author of* A Book for All and None

'Elena Kaufman's scintillating *Love Bites* takes us on a kaleidoscopic trip into the psyches of her characters. By turns darkly humorous and wrenchingly poignant, [*Love Bites*] encapsulates modern love and modern relationships – be they romantic or seeking a soulmate of a non-amorous kind. Some of these love stories bite, others take the bite out of our loneliness and longing to connect with the other. Elena Kaufman's prose shines bright with her half-Alice Munro, half-Dorothy Parker eye for the details that undo us or render us whole.'

Lizzie Harwood, *bestselling author of* Triumph: Collected Stories *and* Xamnesia

'The stories in *Loves Bites* read like confessions overheard in a dark room and are at once bittersweet and delightfully fresh. In them, characters take the unlikeliest of turns to finally embark on journeys that they were always meant to take, and in doing so, explore the different kinds of love life throws in their direction. Kaufman's prose sparkles with dry wit, bewitching the reader into taking these journeys along with her.'

Jing-Jing Lee, author of And Other Rivers *and* If I Could Tell You

'Modern attractions leave their mark in these lyrical, moving and unexpected tales of love, death and everything in between.'

Erinna Mettler, author of Starlings *and* Fifteen Minutes

LOVE BITES

LOVE BITES

ELENA KAUFMAN

To Volker, Benedict, Jonathan, and Leon

Dear Reader,

The book you are holding came about in a rather different way to most others. It was funded directly by readers through a new website: Unbound.

Unbound is the creation of three writers. We started the company because we believed there had to be a better deal for both writers and readers. On the Unbound website, authors share the ideas for the books they want to write directly with readers. If enough of you support the book by pledging for it in advance, we produce a beautifully bound special subscribers' edition and distribute a regular edition and e-book wherever books are sold, in shops and online.

This new way of publishing is actually a very old idea (Samuel Johnson funded his dictionary this way). We're just using the internet to build each writer a network of patrons. Here, at the back of this book, you'll find the names of all the people who made it happen.

Publishing in this way means readers are no longer just passive consumers of the books they buy, and authors are free to write the books they really want. They get a much fairer return too – half the profits their books generate, rather than a tiny percentage of the cover price.

If you're not yet a subscriber, we hope that you'll want to join our publishing revolution and have your name listed in one of our books in the future. To get you started, here is a £5 discount on your first pledge. Just visit unbound.com, make your pledge and type PHANTOM18 in the promo code box when you check out.

Thank you for your support,

Dan, Justin and John
Founders, Unbound

Super Patrons

Alice Jolly
Daniel Kaufman
Robin Kaufman
Rosie Kaufman
David Kaufman
Dan Kieran
Carol Kloevekorn
Clara Kühl
Kate Laktin
Madeleine Lange
Karin Ling
Kester Lovelace
Chris Mack
Nicholas Marshall
Jessica Martin
Hope McIntyre
Oliver Michell
Florian Miro
John Mitchinson
Nicki Moodie
Elliot Neck
Karin & Mat Nichol
Sophie Nicholson
Oliver Niclaus
Liisa Niveri
Neele Peters
Joseph Piergrossi
Justin Pollard
Aaron Riley
Betsy Rosenbaum
David Samson
Smruti Satya
Robyn Schell
Franziska Schneider
Volker Schomerus
Ninon Schubert

John Sexton
A. Srinivasan
Tabatha Stirling
Joerg Teschner
Peter Teuscher
Eibo Thieme
Laura Thompson
Marc Toolan
Writers Unite
Katerina Vasiliou
Barratt Walton
Nicola Watt
Noah Weisbord
Tigi Weisser
Galit Wolfensohn
Mami Yoshida
Henrik Zawischa
Alesia Zuccala

With grateful thanks to Volker Schomerus, who helped to make this book possible.

Synopsis

Love Bites is a collection of thirteen stories set in Europe and North America, tracing the paths of foreigners, drifters and eccentrics. Isolation, loss and a desire for connection are revealed when strangers reach out to other strangers on the streets, in parks, in private spaces. A mysterious older woman and an alienated foreigner, lost on a crowded London street, bond in their search for home. A single woman consults a soothsayer about family problems before he lures her into his own conflict. A former life model and her overgrown son prey on a tourist in a Parisian garden. Interconnected scenes in Montreal, Paris and Toronto are linked by bizarre accidents and those who witness them. A schoolboy, fascinated by his elderly neighbour, adopts him as an absent father. A honeymooning couple in Hawaii, marooned at a remote beach, are forced to strip for their survival. An expat escapes into a new life in Paris until her ex-boyfriend reappears, reminding her of the impact of loss. A woman suffering from dementia is nearly eaten to death by the proliferation of pets running rampant in her home.

Love Bites reveals a kaleidoscope of human experience. Emotionally or geographically displaced, the characters in this collection all have one thing in common: their need to find home.

Contents

PART I

Paris

1

Phantom Appendage

Some people swear by their inner child, but Juliana has something unique. It's lying sideways, resting on her leg: an earthworm, pink and new, with one slit eye staring up at her.

When the phone rang, she was still horizontal on the lumpy sofa. She poked her arm out from under the comforter to prod under a bag of chips, an empty box of cookies, and some glossy French *Galas* strewn over the floor. Paul's voice came from 3,000 miles away.

'My love.'

'Honey, guess what?' she said, her voice cracked with sleep.

'Did I wake you?'

'I grew a penis,' she said.

'What?'

'A dream penis.'

There was a sharp exhalation of breath and then a burst of laughter. 'You're too far away,' he said.

Juliana pushed the curtain of hair from her eyes. 'I haven't been myself since you left.'

'I'm counting the days,' he said and changed the subject to renovations for their new apartment in Seattle, which he'd purchased without her. He'd seen a minimalist style in *Wallpaper* magazine and planned for them to strip off the purple and orange wallpaper, paint every room in a particular shade of beige – no, not beige: milky coffee. They'd buy an antique brass bed and seek out treasures from flea markets because that was her thing. 'Shabby chic' she called it.

'Abandoning the city of lights for the city of rain doesn't seem like a fair exchange,' Juliana said, as she threw the blanket off and rose from the sofa, naked from the waist down. She cradled the phone between ear and shoulder.

'But you said it would be a relief to come home,' he said.

Juliana held her pyjama bottoms up in front of her to thrust her leg in, but got twisted up, fell back onto the sofa, and dropped the phone. She picked it up again, and he was still speaking.

'Don't get all mopey on me. We've gone through this a million times.'

Juliana stood up again, and aimed for her pyjama leg. She was getting cold.

A week ago, they'd moved out of their Parisian apartment, which was on the fifth floor of a walk-up in the 11th district, right beside an award-winning bakery. What they left behind were sun stains on the walls from the outlines of posters: Depardieu and Deneuve in *The Last Metro* and Juliette Binoche in *Blue*. She'd rolled the posters into tubes and sent them with Paul. When she had swept the living room, she found francs lodged under the fireplace; these she washed and polished and packed into her jewellery box. Her herbal tea collection went to friends, and she gave the American Library most of their books, which Paul had considered too heavy and also replaceable. But in Seattle she'd never find a second-hand book on Hilaire Belloc – she knew that much.

Paul had left Paris to start something new, while Juliana stayed behind in a temporary room to finish off something old: her job as a teacher in a high school in the ninth. In one week she and Paul would reunite in an empty room with tubs of paint and stacks of English-language newspapers. But where would she find *Le Figaro*?

'I'm stuck on the Alexandre III Bridge,' Juliana said, 'like one of those cherub statues.'

'You're so dramatic.'

'What? After two years that's news to you?'

'We were lucky to live there at all, but we couldn't stay, you know that. Do you understand how many people were let go from the company? And I only got transferred.'

'Things change,' she said. 'People change.'

'Exactly. Which is why you need to come home – to start a new adventure. It'll be great.'

'Seattle is not my home.' She sank back down on the sofa, was swaddled in a meringue of sheets. The silence grew.

'You still there?' he asked.

'Yep, I'm still here. In Paris.'

'Tell me more about that penis of yours.' His voice had lightened.

'He's a bit shy; otherwise, I'd let him speak for himself.'

'And what would he say?'

Juliana thought about it but she was at a loss. 'Paul, are you naked?' she whispered. 'Like right this minute: are you still in bed, naked?' It would have been six in the morning his time.

'Well, maybe I am,' he said with warmth coming out of him and through the phone line and directly into her sleepy ear.

'If you've got nothing on, then yes,' she said, looking down at her rumpled pyjama bottoms, not daring to touch. She threw the comforter back over her and curled in.

'Well, now I have a friend too,' she whispered.

'Cute. Very cute.'

'He is.'

'Juliana.' His voice was thin now, with a thread of fatigue. 'I've got work. Call you later?'

She patted the comforter into little feathery mounds. Each time one air bubble sank, another popped up. 'The daffodils came out in Luxembourg Gardens. It's gorgeous,' she said. She gathered her hair and pulled it over one shoulder, tugging it down. 'And the picnickers along the Seine... yesterday they were sitting on blankets, drinking wine.' There was a rattling cellophane sound on his side of the line and she held the phone out. When she put it back, a low drone blared.

'Paul? Paul, can you hear me?'

The dial tone clicked in and she gripped the receiver in both hands as if to strangle it, then threw it down and lit a Gitane and lay back on the pullout sofa – which she hadn't bothered to pull out – in the narrow dormitory room. Students of Cardinal Lemoine College had lived here in the 16th century; it was what attracted Juliana to the room. On the ceiling, a spider lowered himself down. She crawled under the duvet and pulled it over her head so that she was in a dark cave. Except for the glowing red ember, it could have been the year 1500 rather than 2000. How many apathetic students had lain in this exact spot, filled up with the same dread? She patted her hand around her thighs, around the borders of her new body part and, without feeling it, knew it was still there. When she'd smoked herself out of the cave and emerged, the phone rang and she let the vibrations hum through her fingers before answering on the third ring.

'Can you hear me?'

'Sure,' she said.

'Juliana, please,' he said. 'We have to move forward.'

'Come back,' she said, and took another drag on the cigarette.

'Are you smoking again?'

'I'll pay for your flight, Paul.'

'I thought you agreed to stop smoking.'

'Forget the stupid job. Come back.'

'You mean the stupid job that pays for you to stay there?'

'I didn't mean… Sorry.'

'Look, it's six in the morning and I've got to get to work. I can't be doing this.'

'It's Sunday,' she said. 'Day of rest?'

'We've got a meeting with head office on Monday. The new guy has to prove himself.'

'Then don't call if you don't have time to talk about it.'

'It's too late. I can't erase everything we set up over here.'

'*You* set up. *You*.' She blew the smoke out as a punch into the receiver, then flicked the cherry off the cigarette. It landed on the woven rug near her bed and began to smoke and she had to use a *Gala* magazine to bat it out. Her neighbour, the troubled one, was shuffling around in her kitchen, washing dishes and rattling cutlery. Juliana's neck was cramping from holding the phone between shoulder and ear.

'What about our friends? Our walks along the Seine? The Beaujolais Nouveau, lemon tarts from our bakery, Sundays at the Louvre?' She could feel herself clawing, peering over that cliff edge she leaned further and further over these days.

'I'll come and get you,' he whispered. 'Would that help?'

She pulled her hair tightly away from her face with her free hand and imagined taking scissors to it.

'I'll cut it off,' she said.

'What are you talking about?'

'Nothing.'

'Listen, I'll find a cheap flight and take a couple of days off work. I'm on my six months' probation but I'll do it if it helps.'

'No,' she said, but tears sprang to her eyes.

'Are you sure?'

She wiped the comforter over her wet cheeks. 'No.'

'What were you doing when I called? It must be three in the afternoon there.'

'At the desk. Studying French,' she lied. Her French books were on the floor, askew with their spines broken.

'OK, then. Can I still expect you next Friday?'

She nodded and lay her head on the pillow.

'Can I?'

'Yes, yes, yes.'

'I miss you, Juliana.'

After hanging up, she grabbed a pillow and hurled it against the wall, where it bounced off the TV and back onto the sofa beside her. The room was too small for tantrums.

That afternoon, she strolled in the sunshine through a maze of quiet Sunday streets. Passing 74 rue du Cardinal Lemoine, where Ernest Hemingway had lived, she blew silent kisses up to his former window. At the top of the hill was Place de la Contrescarpe, with a fountain in the square surrounded by cafés. A homeless man stood fully clothed in the middle of the fountain, splashing water over his head while pigeons cooed around him. His cord pants were torn, and the remnants, tied around his waist with a thick rope, revealed a gaping hole at his crotch, but no matter how Juliana strained to see, she couldn't make out any sign of his mystery peeking out.

She sipped a syrupy espresso at a café on the square that cost her nearly three euros and then wandered down rue Monge, past market stalls brimming with fruits and vegetables. When she turned into Arènes de Lutèce, the remains of a Roman amphitheatre where men and animals had fought fist to hoof, there was a group of men throwing shiny silver pétanque balls along the gravel. Juliana watched how they moved with their birthright between their legs, until one man, who looked to be in his eighties, tipped his hat at her before bowling. When he scored and his friends applauded him, he turned back and bowed to her. All the men looked her way, and she forced a smile. If she'd had the courage, she would have asked them how it felt carrying such sensitive goods around. Instead, she exited the arena and went back down the hill.

At the bottom stood the Jussieu Campus, where Juliana had applied for a job in the English department, but it hadn't worked out. The entrance gate was covered in the same handwritten banners she'd seen on her first visit, protesting rising tuition fees. A lone student, sitting on the ground beside the locked gate, looked up as she passed. Did he recognise her new walk, her cowboy swagger? Juliana looked back over her shoulder, but his head was bowed down in a book.

In the Jardin des Plantes, she walked around the boundaries of newly planted flower beds, kicking up the grey gravel until she tasted dirt in her mouth. When a cloudy curtain passed over the sun, she sought comfort elsewhere.

The mosque on rue Cardinal Lemoine had a café that served tea with real mint leaves, and the place was brimming with photo-snapping tourists, hookah-smoking teens, French literati and white-aproned waiters. The elegant men balanced trays filled with decorative glasses of hot tea and plates of honeyed sweets, while under their arms they carried water pipes with thin hoses dragging behind them like tails. *All this, with the other thing to carry,* she thought. No one looked particularly interested in her: not the giggling teenage boys sharing a pipe, exhaling a swirl of smoke as sharp and fresh as Granny Smith apples; nor the woman at the next table, who was immersed in a book on, as far as she could see, literary symbolism. What if Juliana took off her pants and flung them into the garden? Would the customers look at her then? She could strut around, showing them the secret hermaphrodite she'd become. *Quelle surprise!* She's a sensation, they'd say. If starfish can regenerate arms, then humans can grow missing body parts, she would tell them. The whole day she had been conscious of it resting against her thigh. Men moved differently in this world from women; she saw them shifting and adjusting, as if they were prize horses readying for the race. Juliana tried to imitate by scratching for balls that didn't exist. She lit up another cigarette and smoked away the rest of the afternoon.

That evening, her married friends Cecilia and Maurice took her out for dinner at Chez Bleu in the fifth. They all ordered the moules marinière served with bowls of salty golden fries so hot they burned the roof of her mouth. Cecilia, an expat from Boston, wore a purple silk dress, while Maurice, from La Rochelle, wore a white linen shirt under his motorcycle jacket. She'd never intended to talk about her dream, but after two Kir Royales and four glasses of Chardonnay, it slipped out.

'A penis,' Juliana slurred and leaned back in her chair, stretching her legs out. They stared at her: Cecilia with her chin cradled in her hand, Maurice with his head tilted to the side. His eyes jumped to her chest for a quick second, and she winked at him. Cecilia didn't notice. 'I dreamt I had one. Really, it was wild,' she said, looking directly at him. 'Well, anyway, you know what I mean.'

Maurice folded his arms across his chest and looked away. The idea of it, though, flooded her friend. 'Was it erect?' Cecilia asked, her voice languid from their third bottle.

'*Cherie*, please.' Maurice clapped his hand firmly on his wife's shoulder.

'I didn't have that pleasure,' Juliana said. 'I didn't get to give it a whirl – to pee or anything.'

Cecilia shrugged his hand off and sat up straight, folding her hands on the table. 'So, Juliana, are you (a) trying to assert your masculine side, (b) questioning your sexuality, or (c) feeling impotent?'

It took Juliana a moment to absorb the question. She slurped the dregs from her glass and set it down a little too hard, which made all of their glasses shake. 'Are those my only options?'

Maurice twisted in his seat while he waited for Juliana's answer.

'I mean… couldn't it just be that I'm a hermaphrodite? Simple,' Juliana said.

'Paul should not have left you here alone,' Maurice said. His foot caught Juliana's under the table and she bit her lip. 'That was a grave error,' he said.

Cecilia nodded. 'I agree,' she said.

They exited the restaurant and emerged into the soft evening air tainted with pollution. Traffic sounds filled their ears. Maurice gave her two pecks on the cheeks, and she closed her eyes to smell his woodsy scent. Then he pulled out a pack of cigarettes, lit one and handed it to her before walking away. Cecilia linked her arm in Juliana's and they trailed down the sidewalk behind him.

'He has vagina envy. You should see him at home squeezing into my cocktail dresses. He thinks he's Kate Moss,' Cecilia said.

Juliana laughed so abruptly that it started a coughing fit. She had to hold on to a shop window for support. When she straightened up, she saw the back of Maurice's leather jacket disappearing down the street and Cecilia wiping tears of laughter from her eyes. Cecilia's tiny earrings dangled like little fish hooks, and Juliana reached out and touched one of them. Maurice turned and yelled, '*Cherie*, come! I must rise early to work!'

'Thanks for dinner,' Juliana said. 'And thanks for everything.' Her voice slurred, which made them both giggle again.

'You lush. We'll have to do this again. I'm counting down your dinners here. Only four left.'

'Yeah, let's do the Last Supper thing,' Juliana said, leaning against her friend's shoulder, but then she dropped the cigarette, which bounced against Cecilia's silk dress.

'Careful,' Cecilia said.

Juliana ground out the cigarette and moved in to kiss her friend's cheek until Cecilia's eyes became large blue orbs in front of her. 'On Thursday before I take off?' Juliana said. 'Come alone.' Cecilia looked surprised but agreed. Then Maurice, who was at the end of the street, called out: '*A bientôt*, Juliana.'

'Will you be OK getting home?'

Juliana shrugged. It wasn't the first time she had gotten herself home drunk; she'd hold on to the stone walls for support. They waved each other off, and Juliana stood with her back against a wall, pressing as hard as she could. She watched her friends speed off in their green Citroën, then turned to the fuzzy-looking Metro sign.

The narrow dormitory hall was a long corridor glimmering with shadows from the high windows. Street light shone through them onto the uneven tiles of the floor. The only human sounds she ever heard in the building came from the woman next door, who had been arguing with someone on the telephone for the past three nights. In her room, the sofa bed was still folded up and the curtains left open. She kept the lights off but fingered the remote so the cool blue flicker of the TV shimmied up her walls. She tripped over her French books and stubbed her toe on the coffee table and screamed out *Merde!* Sitting down on the sofa, she stripped off her black dress and lay under the feathery comforter. It was her third sleep alone. She nudged the phone off its cradle so that the dial tone was a lullaby. Her fingers punched in his memorised number. It rang only once. 'Are you still awake?' she asked. There was a deep groan. '*Quelle heure est-il?*' His voice was full of what she loved: cigarettes and booze. Juliana laid her cold hands on her warm breasts.

'Maurice. Maurice,' she said. 'Are you alone?'

'*S'il te plaît*. Please, Juliana.'

'Are you crying?' she said. Her own eyes got itchy and blurry at the same time. On TV a muted chef was speed-chopping green onions with a long knife.

'Did I shock you at the restaurant with my story?'

'You had too much to drink again and you were not careful.'

There was a muffled sound on the other line, and she heard a door being closed.

'Maurice?'

'You, *mon amour*, are so sexy that I wouldn't care if you had four eyes. But a penis? Disgusting.'

'I'll miss you. I mean it.'

'I'm just an old man to you,' he whispered. 'It's all I ever was.'

'No, that's not it.'

'*Au revoir.*'

The dial tone rang in her ears.

An hour later, Juliana was still awake and staring at the shadows on the ceiling. In her sodden head was a kaleidoscope of shifting colours and sounds and memories. The TV was off and the blankets were kicked onto the carpet. The heavy air in the room smelled of dust and dry wood from the ceiling beams. Juliana tried to call Paul but he wasn't picking up; she imagined him sitting at his new desk, doing important things for English-speaking people. The legal firm was on the 14th floor in downtown Seattle. He would be gliding around the spacious department, his reflection beaming in the shiny surfaces, while in her room she was held captive by dark wooden beams and a woven straw mat, an uneven ceiling, and precariously wired light fixtures. Every time the neighbour took a shower, the tap in the kitchen turned from a flow to a trickle. Here, they were all connected, these lives that never intersected in the hallway. Three steps away from the bed was the table where she ate, wrote and played solitaire. On it, the candle Paul bought at the artisanal market was now lopsided, half burnt with its long black wick drooping down.

It didn't take much to pull herself from her nest and to light that candle; she stared at the flame until her eyes were full of dancing stars. With blurry vision and her head swimming with wine, she grabbed her French exercise book and held it up to the small flame – all of those conjugations she'd spent months on became hot and bright. The edges of paper curling at *à vous* and *à tu* and then — with a crackle, rush, and blaze, the book fell out of her hand and dropped onto her sofa bed in flames. The shock of it made her leap back and she watched as her pillow melted open and set silent fireworks of feathers into the room. Everything sparkled golden.

No sounds but the crackling fire could be heard. Some escaping feathers alighted onto the bed. Then the slow burn of Paul's letters and her own writing: everything she fed it made it louder and stronger until Juliana's remembered friend was pulled upright to attention. Now she put her hand around her phantom appendage and it was there. She knew it, she felt it. Now she hopped from one foot to the other to avoid the rising heat from the woven mat, her eyes so full of light it was a wonder to behold.

2

Sunday in the Park with Betty

The sloping lawns in the Luxembourg Gardens are off limits to everyone but the gardener. For their protection, a short man in an oversized uniform is on patrol. His French is difficult to understand, but his foot, planted every so often on the low railings in front of whoever is there – sunbathers, readers and daydreamers – is a reminder not to cross that iron line. What is forbidden to everything but the eye is a green oasis mowed in thick, alternating stripes with the centrepiece a stone Apollo, naked, with his arms and eyes raised to the sky. It's a museum of nature with velvety grass framed by sculptured flower beds, chestnut trees humming with birds, and everything just out of reach.

Jonathan admired the view spread out before him. He sat in one of the park's iron chairs that were lined up side to side along the edges of the green lawns. He had stuck his thumb in his book, though, to hold his place, ever since she'd come over to sit beside him.

'The English do not speak French to us when we go there,' she said. 'They refuse, *mais* when they come here they can speak French. I have heard those tourists; they are not very good but I have heard them speak French *et alors* they will not speak with us in their own country.'

'That's too bad,' he said.

The woman adjusted her fedora, tucking strands of wiry hair back into the black hat, which was covered with cottony fluff from the shedding trees. She called out to a middle-aged man who sat in the next row of chairs: '*Les Anglais sont mauvais, non?*'

'*Oui, Maman. C'est vrai,*' the man replied. He was wearing a private-schoolboy's outfit: blue blazer with short trousers and a white shirt buttoned up to his chin. He also wore a black bow tie and sported a black moustache. Nestled into a chair with pages of newspaper spread over his lap, he reminded Jonathan of a Botero sculpture: rotund, smooth and benign. The hatted woman turned her attention back to Jonathan. '*You* are not English,' she said.

'I'm Canadian. From British Columbia.'

'Ah, so you are British and hiding in *le Canada,*' she said, and then told him he had a funny accent but still she would consider him for what he was: a French cousin after all. She wanted to know if it snowed six months of the year and if bears lived in his backyard. Since nobody had taken an interest in Jonathan since his arrival in Paris, he happily explained Canada's drastic weather patterns and *The Farmer's Almanac* predictions before she cut in.

'You are lucky not to be *le vrai Anglais*, from the Grande Bretagne,' she said. '*C'est très cher là-bas.* Do you know how much we paid for a hotel in Kent when we arrived?'

'Kent? But it's much cheaper there than London,' he said.

'And they would not serve us breakfast after ten, can you *comprehend*? We had no breakfast for one week as they would not serve it after ten. And who gets up before ten? *C'est incroyable, non?*' She pulled up her nylons, which had slumped like beige earthworms around her ankles.

Three thin German women, sitting on the chairs to their right, chatted together with fluttering hands. On the left side, a teenage girl sitting in a boy's lap kissed his closed eyelids.

'Then, we had to go to an office to look up his grandmother's name, to track her down, you see, and did that office not suddenly disappear? We spent the money on this trip, with the ferry across – oh, that dreaded ferry – only to find no office, no more. How was he to find his grandmother? They did not think of that, oh no. You see, he has the dual citizenship. His father: British – I cannot tell you who he is, *non, non* – and he has never met his grandmother. *C'est tragique, non?* And then we go back *encore*, another time on that ferry to be sick again. We French are, how to say… sensitive?'

Jonathan pulled his thumb completely out of his book, shutting the pages on *Anatomy of a Naval Disaster: The 1746 French Naval Expedition to North America* by James Pritchard.[1] The sun strained through the chestnut leaves and cast long shadows on his feet. He rested his eyes on the green lawn and on the statue of Apollo: strong, still, quiet. 'This time we found another office, but would you not know it? They could not help us, and those English are so rude! What a nightmare, that place!' she said. '*Ah, je préfère Paris. J'adore! Je ne quitterai Paris, jamais.* Never. *Comprenez?*'

Her voice had risen and the kissing couple stopped nuzzling and stared at them. The German women looked over and Jonathan shrugged at them and turned back to her. 'The people here are charming,' he said, thinking of the blonde chambermaid who'd greeted him in the corridor that morning. 'The women are absolutely—'

'*Non*, we have a *joie de vivre* that you will not find in those British,' she said. When she threw her head back and laughed, her fedora flipped off, landing on the ground. Most of her hair was thin and white, but the ends were dyed black. She grabbed the hat and plopped it back on. 'No, I rest here. This is the best city. The best city in the world, *n'est-ce pas?*'

Jonathan nodded and stretched out his legs, pushing the fine gravel away from his heels. Glancing over at her son, he caught the man staring. They locked eyes until the son ducked behind his *Figaro*. High-heeled steps coming up the path were dainty and measured: a woman with silky hair down to her waist approached and Jonathan smiled at her. She smiled too as she passed.

'Yes, Paris is a good city; I find it very aesthetic here,' Jonathan said. 'Paris is the most photographed city in the world, you know.'

The woman nodded and pulled her chair closer to him. 'Photographed, *oui, oui*. But photos of *le Canada, c'est incroyable*, with Indians and igloos, *non?* And you sleep in ice houses, *non?*' She raised her eyebrows up and held them there, waiting.

'You're thinking about the Inuit who live way up north, but no, in the cities we live in apartments. And we have heating. Like you.' He leaned back in his chair, yawned and closed his eyes. It was quiet

1. Pritchard, James. 'Epilogue.' Anatomy of a Naval Disaster. Montreal: MQUP, 2011. Print.

for a moment. The woman's son crept up beside them and knelt over Jonathan who felt a warm breath on his face. When Jonathan's eyes flashed open to see the moustached man over him, the man stumbled back and grabbed his mother's hand.

'He has never seen a Canadian. *Jamais*,' she said.

Jonathan stared the guy down until she shooed her son back.

'I saw on ARTE channel, an *emission* on *le Canada*. I saw people like you in an ice house, so it is true, *la vérité*.'

'Now that you mention it,' Jonathan said, 'Quebec does have an ice hotel, but only in the winter and it's very expensive. I suspect it's only a fad.'

The son leaned over his mother and tugged at a long hair growing out of her chin.

'*Arrête tes bêtises!*' she said, pushing him away.

The son walked back to his chair and plopped down. She took out some hand cream and massaged her bony fingers. Jonathan opened up his book again and reread the same line.

'The ice hotel. How interesting, how charming,' she said. 'I shall visit your homeland. When my royalties come from the Matisse painting, I shall surprise my son.'

'The Matisse painting?' Jonathan said, looking up from his book.

'*Oui, bien sûr.* The painting. The money. I have not had *l'argent* to buy a gift for my little boy, my Simon. For the birthday.'

'How old is your little boy?' Jonathan said, looking over at the moustached man.

'Yesterday was the birthday. *Le bonheur.* I cooked a *gâteau au chocolat meringué* and Simon got forty-nine.'

'Forty-nine, eh?'

A summer breeze swept over them and lit under the woman's black dress to puff it up like a tent in a storm. The breeze blew through the chestnut trees and ruffled the wings of pigeons, cooing and shifting. Then, a bullet dropped from the leafy branch above and hit her. The woman winced and brought her hand up to her eyes, and after a moment looked up at the bird. '*Merde!*' she cried out.

'*Oui Maman, c'est la merde*,' Simon said, baring all his teeth. The woman looked at her fingers, covered in soft beige goo, then up at the tree, then back at her hand again. Jonathan pulled out a package of tissues and held them out.

'*Oh monsieur, que c'est gentil,*' she said. 'Thank you most kindly.'

'My name is Jonathan, by the way,' he told her.

'*Enchanté. Je m'appelle* Betty.'

'Betty,' he repeated. 'What were you saying about Matisse, Betty?'

'I say nothing about that man, nothing worth to say.' Betty scrubbed her skin with the tissues then wiped the sides of her mouth with them. '*Oh, merde encore!*' She threw the tissues down and rose to stamp them into the gravel path with the heel of her shoe.

The German women beside them stifled laughter. Jonathan looked down at his book and read the same line for the third time: 'Despite France's military position on the Continent and Britain's unchallenged preponderance at sea, both the whale and the elephant were anxious to come to terms.'

Betty went over to her son, who was eating a sandwich. She snatched it from him and took a bite. 'I know what you imagine,' she called out with a mouthful of bread. 'He is little Monsieur Matisse, what you call "junior" in America.'

'Canada,' Jonathan said.

'Junior Matisse? *Non.* It's simply false, no matter what they say. I could not lie about such things to a nice foreigner. *Non,* his papa is British but you are not the first to think such thoughts but *c'est pas vrai. Bien sûr,* Junior knows the artists and they know him because of me,' she said. 'He is what you call a small star turning, turning in a big sky, *n'est-ce pas?*'

The German women beside Jonathan rose and collected their shopping bags. One smiled at Jonathan as she linked arms with her friends and walked away. Betty watched them go, muttering '*Les Allemands*' under her breath.

'What was that?' asked Jonathan. His grandparents were German.

'*Les Allemands,*' she said, shaking her head so that her fleshy neck wobbled. 'The Occupation.' From her purse, she pulled out a black and white photo of two young women. '*Regardez.* I have the suit and my sister has the military uniform, *voyez?*' She gave him the photo.

'Your sister was in the army?' he asked. Her sister was hugging a tree trunk and staring intensely into the camera.

'The occupation,' she said. 'We lost our family. We had to fight – for ourselves.'

Simon squirmed in his seat. *'Maman, s'il te plaît,'* he whined, but Betty turned her back on him and told Jonathan how she had modelled for painters, often for Matisse and Picasso. While Jonathan studied her photographed image, she dug into an oversized purse and with her gold-ringed fingers pulled out a postcard reproduction of a painting: *Odalisque in Red Pants* which portrayed a bare-breasted woman sitting beside a vase of flowers.

'C'est moi. I posed at La Ruche, you have heard? The colony of artists at Montparnasse? Modigliani was there; what a scoundrel! I was not thin enough for that man. He wanted the – how you say? – *maigre*, meagre girls with hunger. *Ça, ce n'est pas moi.* Not me, *comprenez?'*

Jonathan nodded and watched her reach back into her purse to find a postcard of Matisse's *Decorative Figure on an Ornamental Background.* *'Celle là, c'est bien moi,'* she said and watched Jonathan's eyes widen. The next card, dog-eared and stained, was from a gallery showing in Berlin of her and another young woman sitting together. *'La blonde* is *Italienne.* I don't remember the name,' Betty said. 'She married an aristocrat.' In the painting, two young women sat back to back.

'I know this one,' Jonathan said. 'I remember seeing this one.' He flipped through the cards while Betty returned to her chair.

'Picasso loved *les filles.* He adored the women. He was *passionné,'* she said.

'And Matisse? What was he like?' Jonathan asked.

'Each man is a little island. Matisse kept alone and he already had the great love. He was not interested in us, the models. *Vous savez, les deux sont vraiment différents.'*

'How were they different?'

Betty shrugged, and then told him of her privileges as a former artists' model: a lifetime pass into any museum in France. Did he know there was a Matisse exhibition at the Musée du Luxembourg right now? She grimaced. 'It's only drawings, the sketches. But no paintings, none to see. And not me. Can you understand I am not there?'

'I studied drawing at art school,' Jonathan told her. 'Picasso and Matisse were masters of the form.'

She whipped her head up. 'You? You are an artist?' her voice became high-pitched.

'I studied art but I wouldn't call myself an artist,' he said. 'More of a photographer.'

'So you are the one. You!' Betty stood up and twirled in her shimmering black skirt. Some fluff fell from the tree onto her shoulder.

'*Quelle chance.* How fated we meet,' she said.

Jonathan sat upright. 'I went into graphic design,' he said quickly. 'I'm not an actual artist.'

'You, I have waited for,' Betty said. She pointed at him with a crooked, shaky finger and dumped the contents of her purse onto his lap: reproductions, photos, drawings, gallery postcards, lipsticks, cigarettes and a half-eaten bread roll. Then she dropped her empty purse onto the ground and ran over to her son, swiped the newspaper from his hands and whispered in his ear. Mother and son looked with sidelong glances at Jonathan and then Betty began a slow but direct path back towards him, pointing her toes like a ballerina as she walked. Jonathan put each object back into her purse, including the bread roll. When he looked up, Betty had nearly reached him. A cell phone went off behind her and Simon pulled it out of his pocket as if it were a bomb.

'*Maman!*' he cried and when she turned he tossed it to her. Betty caught it and held it like a microphone at her chin, yelling: 'We are by the statue. *Tu sais où elle est.* Yes, beside the big grass.'

Jonathan shoved his Paris map and book into his backpack.

'Bring your paints and come quick!' she screamed into the phone. '*Enfin! Oui, je te jure, c'est vrai!*'

When Jonathan rose from his chair and slung his backpack over his shoulder his book fell out. Betty lunged for it, clasping it to her bosom. Jonathan held out his hand but she slipped it under her arm.

'You *must* paint us, monsieur,' she said. 'It is your duty. *Moi,* Simon *et* another model telephones. Now she comes.'

'Oh no,' he said. 'I only took one course a long time ago. I'm a pho-tographer, I said.'

'Please! My friend takes paint for you. All you need to make the masterpiece.' Betty picked up her purse.

Simon approached and said: 'I bring *le journal*?'

'I have to go,' Jonathan said. 'I have an appointment. It was a plea-sure meeting you. Both of you.' He reached out tentatively for his book but she wouldn't let it go.

'It is your duty – your calling,' she said to Jonathan and slipped the book into her purse. 'Here you are and we meet like the fate, and now is the time for our final, *nôtre dernier portrait*. The sunshine is less now and it is time. *Attendez.*'

Betty pulled her son by the hand so they stumbled over the iron railing – that forbidden boundary – and onto the lawn. People around them looked up and stared. The kissing girl on her boyfriend's lap giggled.

'Betty! Betty?' Jonathan called out. 'I don't think it's a good idea.' He looked around for the guard and, for once, the man was not in sight. 'You're not supposed to be in there,' he whispered. 'It's forbid-den.'

Betty and Simon dragged their feet over the lawn, making tracks in the pristine green. When they got to the centre of it, Betty stripped the clothes off her son and then took her own clothes off, including her hat. Jonathan held a hand over his mouth. Betty placed their clothes and her purse beside the statue and they moved into what looked like a rehearsed pose. Simon lay on his side, cradled in the grass at his mother's feet, but propped on an elbow to read the newspaper open in front of him. Betty stood just behind him and stretched her arms above her in the air, so that her flesh strained over her ribcage. Her breasts were thin and pendulous and when she dropped her arms down they nearly touched her navel. She took up a stance from one of the reproductions on a postcard: hands on hips, feet set apart, and her head turned to profile with her chin tilted up. Simon turned the page of the newspaper and then they both remained completely still.

Jonathan took out his camera, and through the lens witnessed the wind shuffling through their hair and a sparrow swooping over

Betty's head. The first shot was nearly perfect but then he took another, and another – aiming to capture this truth. Sunbathers, readers and daydreamers gazed on them with their naked eyes: these flesh-coloured relics from another time. Behind Jonathan, an elderly woman, with grey hair done up in a chignon, arrived and joined them, sitting at the son's feet, which made a balanced composition. Jonathan spent the rest of the afternoon behind his lens, capturing lost time.

3

Triumvirate

1. Montreal. Winter.

The snow is, as expected, up to the knees. The woman doesn't know yet about global warming or the tropical times to come. She takes careful steps along boulevard de Maisonneuve, admiring the dazzling banks of white, ploughed to the sides. She could have skied to work; it had crossed her mind when she watched the neighbour leave on hers.

The woman flips her collar up and the lining – a slash of red – is revealed. A woollen scarf, a recent gift, is knotted around her neck, while a thinner one winds around her upper chest like a mummy's wrap. The woman doesn't feel the chill because she's thinking of him, waiting at the café with a cigarette perched on his lips. Waiting for heaping bowls of pasta, red wine, spicy kisses and busy fingers.

He had approached her in a queue at the bank, of all places. She was purchasing a GIC, a government insured certificate, while he, he later confessed, was paying an overdraft. He overspent on everything: money, time, love. The man was deeply in debt.

That first morning she awoke with his fingers in her mouth and on her pillow, her silky black hair mixed with his salt and pepper. He was expected at a conference in Toronto that weekend, but skipped out of it. He was a man who knew his priorities.

Yes, she'd noticed his ring and still accepted his invitation for coffee, which led to dinner and later, a drink. She welcomed what came after too. Yes, she most definitely saw the gold band, and no, she didn't have a problem with it.

And so on for eight months. No talk of making their routine permanent, or skipping town together, or any promises of any kind. It was pure, encapsulated, undisguised pleasure.

As she turns the corner, a gust of wind knocks her sideways and she struggles to catch her breath. There it is, unravelled before her: another story. An indelible image, but not a photograph, a painting or a film; this cannot be rewound, erased or destroyed. This isn't caused by internal mishap: seconds lost while tuning a radio, or hands off the steering wheel, or an uncontrollable sneeze. No, this is about snow and ice and Mother Nature taking a life.

So there it is: crushed steel, smoking engines, red-streaked snow and a rescue worker with a giant's pliers, ripping a door off one of the cars. Using the tool like a can opener. Inside is a man dressed (prophetically) in black, with his head flung back on the seat and a line of blood traced down his chin.

Twisted metal parts steam in big hills of snow. Or little mountains of snow. Whichever way she looks at it, it doesn't matter because there it is: red on black on white.

She staggers into a pharmacy and finds a chair to sit on before she falls. Red lights blink on the heart-monitor machine and she slips a narrow finger into a black plastic hood and watches the screen flash while a message appears:

Unable to read heart rate. Try again.

She springs out of the chair, paces up and down different aisles in the pharmacy looking for something to hold on to, something to ground her. She fills a shopping basket with items she will need when she goes home and calls in sick: five bottles of water, eight boxes of aspirin, ten boxes of Kleenex, five packs of gum, five chocolate bars and three packs of cookies. She weaves up and down the aisles, takes another basket and piles in hair products, nail polish, makeup remover; checks the shopping list in her hand and sees an address instead: Fornicello's Italian Restaurant.

Outside, she lowers her head and squints at the ground to follow a blur of white, just enough definition to stay on the path. The sirens have stopped their wail and it is far too quiet. The plastic bags cut into her gloved hands. She hears the man from the red car groaning as he's lifted onto a stretcher. But the other car, the silver one, was abandoned by the rescuers. There it is: the licence plate, the French flag on the bumper, and inside, his salt-and-pepper head thrown back on the seat.

2. Paris. Summer.

An elderly man, a classical composer, dressed in a cream linen suit hugs a lamp post at Place du 18-Juin-1940. His head presses against it while his lower body pulls away. The loose skin on his neck wobbles and his fingers strum the post, as if he's playing an instrument. The American girl thinks he could be drunk on lunch wine. She's seen the French drinking at their meals, even in the middle of the day. She watches him a little longer and notices his body change. Grasping the pole, he pulls himself taller and his chest expands, looking as if he's about to dance a final pirouette in a ballet, before he releases the pole. Gravity calls and his body reels backwards into the street.

The pedestrian light flashes green, but her legs are too slow, and she has already missed catching him before his head hits the street. She kneels and others do the same. A man in a dark suit yells out, '*Appelez le SAMU! Vite! Vite!*' Three people on mobile phones hesitate. Then: ring. Ring. Ring.

The man comes to with glazed-over eyes. He's had a stroke, a brain attack.

A discarded croissant lies near his head, and at his feet, an empty bottle of Evian. He looks up at the clear blue sky and is transported back to his youth, lying in a field in Toulouse, watching cloud animals pass by. Humming fills his ears.

People hover nearby and the summer sun breaks through to land on his flaccid cheek. The ambulance's soprano sound comes closer. The young girl leans over and smiles; her American high-school French is insufficient, so she strokes his hair instead, avoiding the nearly black blood streaming out the back of his head. She takes off her thin sweater and lays it over his chest. A pigeon pecks at the croissant.

The bystanders turn to one another. *Did you see it? How did it happen? Where's the ambulance? Oh, just there. Look, it's stuck in traffic.* Its high-pitched whine makes people cower and she puts her hands over the stricken man's ears.

He struggles to focus on her face leaning over him, but sees spinning colours and patterns around her head – like looking through a kaleidoscope. The composer feels the warm sun on his face and the weight on his eyelids. When he closes them, he hears his most recent symphony and smells mulled wine and fruit.

'Monsieur? Monsieur!' the girl cries.

He feels her patting hand and remembers her chocolate-brown eyes and thinks about his wife, whom he hasn't seen for five long years.

Witnesses witness. The ambulance screams like a wailing wife, furiously, while a rescue worker leaps out of the vehicle and weaves through traffic. A woman with a flower-patterned scarf wrapped around her head bends beside the American girl, taps on the man's lips and places a makeup mirror under his nose.

'*Trop tard. C'est trop tard*,' she tells the girl, squeezing her shoulder. '*Pauvre lui*,' she announces to the crowd, then covers her mouth with a thick hand.

The young girl waits until the rescue workers arrive, and then she moves away. The siren cuts out as the vehicle pulls up and blocks a lane of traffic. She watches as they hoist the man onto a stretcher and slot him into the back of the ambulance. On the street is a small patch of blood in the shape of a cloud. The crowd has dispersed as if...? As if. But there is nothing else to do.

She takes hold of the lamp post. The woman in the flower-patterned scarf picks up a paper bag of postcards and hands it back to the girl. The girl waits for the woman to leave before letting go of the bag; her messages fall away.

After a few minutes, she follows the sidewalk until it turns the corner to an outdoor café on Rue de Rennes. The girl collapses into an empty chair and grasps the sugar dispenser. The waiter brings her a café crème and the heat from the porcelain cup emanates into her skin. He brings her a glass of water, then more coffee, then more water.

When she asks him for a cigarette, he leaves his own pack on the table and she smokes until there's nothing left.

3. Toronto. Fall.

A Japanese man runs for the subway at King Street. The tinny announcement warning passengers to step away from the doors fades away on the nearly empty platform. The man leaps anyway and the doors, as they're meant to, close.

The blonde passenger sees him first, and she recoils at the sight: a face squished between rubber stoppers while his body flails helplessly behind on the platform, his briefcase swinging in his hand. The man is silent; there's not much he can say when his mouth is forcibly closed. His eyes search like a fish looking out of its tank, or a bird out of its cage. This is what he sees:

A woman with fluffy, blonde hair and raised eyebrows, who looks like Marilyn Monroe: so pretty. Beside her, a man in a striped Hugo Boss suit: the same one he owns. And a boy with a white face like a geisha, and long, greasy, black hair covering one eye.

The woman: studies the trapped man's cheeks, so compressed that they meet his nose. His black hair pokes up like needles and reminds her of a blowfish. She turns away to stifle a giggle.

The geisha boy: whispers a profanity under his breath. The guys' eyes are bulging like they're going to pop out, like in that horror film on YouTube.

The businessman: his mouth drops open. He once read in *The Star* about a man clinging to the outside of a subway car through the tunnel to rescue his dog, who had jumped on without him. This trapped man's face turns from white to red.

The businessman moves first but only a split second before his neighbours. Three of them rush the doors and it takes their six arms to pry them, with much effort, open. The rubber stoppers release the man's face with a wet, sucking plunger sound. The Japanese man stumbles into the car with wild eyes and falls into a seat but leaps up again. Thick black lines, like tire tracks, run down his face.

When the Marilyn asks him if he's all right, he turns away to stagger down the aisle. Passengers look up from their books and bags, see the vertical stripes down his cheeks and look back at one another.

Marilyn, businessman and geisha boy stay at the end of the subway car, where he left them. She adjusts her hair, the man clears his throat and the boy shuffles. No one makes a move.

The man smiles at the woman. The woman looks at the boy. The boy gives a low whistle back to the man. They stand, a triumvirate, giving their silent verdict.

The woman wonders how long it will take before the rescued man notices the evidence on his cheeks. Will it be in the bathroom at work, or in his reflection in an office building on the way in, or because of a polite colleague? How long will it take before he can't deny that this happened and decides to find the three of them and thank them?

But it will be too late by then. His rescuers will have been swallowed up in the morning rush hour by the time he realises his mistake.

4

Lost Time

Rue de Rivoli was crowded with shoppers, who rushed along the cobblestone streets to duck under awnings when the rain poured down. Carmen carried a fluorescent yellow umbrella and the two of them continued on, stepping over gathering puddles, while Graham's leather shoes darkened at the toes. He described his minimally furnished apartment in Amsterdam: a bed, a table and chairs, the walls left intentionally blank.

'I'm anti-art,' he told her. 'I prefer the sun and shadows patterning my walls.'

She walked ahead of him and called back. 'How did you end up in Amsterdam?'

'Pardon?' he said.

Her voice was muffled by the shushing of water under the wheels of cars and the pattering feet of pedestrians. '*Why Amsterdam?*' she shouted.

Graham caught up to her. 'You didn't read my emails?'

She sped up, pretending not to hear, then turned into a narrow side street and stumbled on a cobblestone. He reached out to steady her.

'Damn shoes,' she said, and, looking up at him, noticed the strands of wet hair stuck to his cheek.

'I got a placement from Toronto to work with Greenpeace. That was two years ago... I thought you'd at least read my emails?'

'Well, that's what you always wanted,' she said.

'I did write to you about it.'

'Look at you: you're getting soaked,' she said, stepping around a fallen ice-cream cone and squeezing between boutique windows and parked cars. 'I was surprised when you called,' she yelled back. 'I had no idea you were coming to Paris.'

Graham grabbed her arm, stopped her. 'Carmen,' he said. The rain fell on his shoulders, seeping through his thin coat. He pulled her under a department-store awning to wait for the storm to subside. The sheets of sideways rain made them press in closer to each other, and also to the others taking shelter. Carmen told him about the Eiffel Tower light show projected onto her ceiling every night and how it was better than any painting she'd seen in the Orsay – even better than the impressionists. She jammed her shaking hands into her pockets.

'Are the lights for something special? A celebration?' he asked.

'Well, it was lit up for the millennium New Year's Eve party, but the Parisians liked it so much they made it permanent,' she said. Her voice was breathless.

'Impressive.'

'It is. It starts at dusk and sparkles every hour on the hour for 10 minutes until midnight.'

She didn't tell him she normally fell asleep at 10 or that she barely went out in the evenings, having cut her social life down to the occasional coffee date.

The Eiffel Tower lights were imposing in her *chambre de bonne* — a maid's room under the roof. She'd prop the skylight open on its iron rod and stick her head out when she felt too claustrophobic. The view was of hundreds of red-brick chimneys jutting out every which way, with fluttering pigeons perched and cooing. At night, with this light show, the structures would shift; what was once stable became fragmented and hard to place. No wonder she felt dizzy most of the time. Her friends back home thought where she lived was exotic, even though she explained over and over that it was only a tiny room under the roof with 10 flights of stairs and no elevator. Those Canadians couldn't comprehend a shortage of space, or the concept of living in a closet. Nine square metres was the legal minimum for each person; it was a state-given right held over from Napoleonic law. But some landlords found a way around the rule, based on overpopulation and the numbers of naive foreigners flooding in. Carmen's room was eight square meters; she supposed maids never had, nor would have, the luxury of space. Her friends didn't understand why, with a degree in French literature, she was teaching English grammar to high-school students who cared only to memorise swear words. Her friends imagined a different reality for her: eating cheese and pastries, drinking wine, walking up the Champs-Élysées. Being a *flâneur*. That's what they would do if they were fortunate enough to be there; they had told her so. Living in Paris was about finding your fortune, creatively and financially. They offered Carmen weekly suggestions:

— Become a writer. Follow Hemingway's trail.

— Go to cooking school and learn how to make soufflés. Remember *Breakfast at Tiffany's?*

— Become an art historian. There are all those museums.

— Give tours of Paris to English visitors.

— Learn French design, or if you're serious about making money, take photos of the Metro entrances and scan them onto T-shirts.

— Become a film-maker. Think Jean Renoir! Louis Malle! Agnès Varda!

— Study cheese. Become a cheese connoisseur.

— A sommelier, yeah, then you'd have a good excuse to drink wine every day.

— Buy an apartment and rent it out to foreigners.

— Be a nanny to the rich and famous, but don't let the kids put you off.

— Find a French sugar daddy, yeah, that's the easiest solution. Then you can get your papers and I can come and live with you.

Her closest friend, Toni, offered the last suggestion on a regular basis: 'Get yourself one of those sexy Gitanes-smoking men. They know how to hold a door open for a girl. Not like the hockey fanatics over here who only know how to hold their beers.'

In any case, Toni and others lived vicariously through her, so that on the weekends she felt obliged to do some touristy things. And she admitted she did enjoy some of them, or simply the act of going outside, which helped her to breathe more easily. But when the dizzy spells started in the classroom and she had to hold on to a desk and look at the floor until they passed, Carmen went to a doctor.

'I'm not pregnant.'

'Are you *absolument* positive?'

'Absolutely.'

'Perhaps you forgot the protection? Just once in the heat of a moment, is it correct?'

'I'm positively, absolutely sure that didn't happen. I promise.'

Then there was a beat, a pause, while he looked at her face, her chest, her clothing.

'*Alors*,' he said. 'You have an iron deficiency. We do the blood test.'

After seeing the doctor, her nightmares returned. The ones where she leaned over Escher-esque staircases going up, down and sideways, like an interminable rollercoaster ride. Other times, she was pushed by an unseen hand down a mountain, to trip over boulders and tree branches, never reaching stable ground. That one reminded Carmen of her girlhood, when she'd balanced, knees bent, in the centre of a seesaw, just waiting to flinch and fall.

'Here we are,' Carmen said when they arrived at the tiny bistro: *Café Au Temps Perdu.*

'Lost time?' Graham said.

She nodded. They were seated at a cosy table in the corner, beside a window onto the street. She thought eating would be a distraction, but he went and brought up the topic of children before the waiter even arrived.

'My girlfriend doesn't want kids,' he said, picking at wax from the candle between them. 'She thinks the world is overpopulated as it is.'

Carmen's heart jumped. So the day wasn't what she'd thought. 'What about adoption?' She tried to keep her voice even and clear in tone. 'Would she consider that?'

'No. Most people have to adopt abroad, and she thinks that taking a child from its heritage is just another form of colonisation.' He sipped a mouthful of red wine and savoured it. All the while looking at her.

Carmen hesitated, flushed and looked down. 'Oh, I see.'

So he was out of the question now. If she had stayed behind three years ago, there would be a child sitting between them in a restaurant somewhere in Toronto. Babies were not political to her, but a natural part of life. She only had to find a new boyfriend now to make that happen again, when she was good and ready. Or just ready. She wondered how socially conscious Graham's girlfriend was and if she actually donated to Oxfam or Save the Children or any of those other organisations. Did they have a good relationship? Did they have good sex? Did she have perfect, shiny hair?

Outside the café, the windows were streaked with rain, and inside they were fogged as if in a greenhouse. Carmen patted down her frizzy hair, and Graham used his napkin to wipe a circle on the window so they could watch people passing by. He drank the wine, served in globular glasses and smelling of strawberries and freshly chopped wood, and she copied him because it gave her something to do. Every time he raised his glass, she avoided looking at the backs of his hands, at his broad fingers, strong knuckles and ropy veins. The hands that had once held her quivering breasts.

The waiter appeared with steaming bowls of French onion soup, and she dipped baguette into the salty broth. Then, generous portions of quiche Lorraine arrived with crisp green salads covered in a lemony vinaigrette. She kept her hands busy with knife, fork, spoon, napkin, water and wine to stop herself from reaching out and putting a hand on his. It was too late for that. But then she ate too quickly and burned her mouth. For dessert, she ordered a *tarte aux cerises* with vanilla ice cream, which cooled her tongue. He drank two espressos, and she tried to remember if she'd ever seen him drink coffee in their five years together. Beside them, an elderly man lit up a cigarette and blew smoke rings that wafted up and dissolved over their heads.

'Do you still smoke?' she asked.

'I quit a year ago,' he said, looking up at the next cloud of smoke.

'Congratulations.' She hoped that came out sincerely.

'Yeah, I took up jogging. Can you believe it? I'm running marathons now.' The corners of his lips were stained with wine.

'That's amazing. You must be in great shape.'

'I am,' he said placing his hand on his chest. 'Doc says I have a healthy heart.'

Carmen noticed the hand was a bit off target and a rush of adrenaline went through her, and then her eyes were tearing and she was getting up, pushing her chair back and wrestling into her coat. She threw 30 euros down on the table.

'Don't you want your change?' he asked, but she didn't hear him since she was already at the door.

Outside, the fog blanketed the buildings in an undulating curtain of grey.

'I'm sorry,' she said. 'I needed air.' Her mouth was getting tired from smiling whenever he looked at her. The arch of his long neck and the way he scratched his tousled hair made her want to escape to a museum or a movie.

They spent nearly two more hours together, and as long as they were walking, she relaxed. The heavy rain turned into a light drizzle as they made their way along the Quai des Tuileries to the Pont Neuf. Daylight faded and the city became illuminated in the fog, light by light, jewel by jewel. On the Pont Neuf, they peered over at a passing Bateaux Mouche full of tourists with umbrellas splayed open. Those with rain jackets were hunched over with their hoods up, all except for one man who stood tall with his foot up on the stern, one hand holding his small hat down. He waved at them.

'Check out this guy with the beret,' Graham said, and leaned over the rail to wave back.

'He's probably a tourist from California.' Her laughter came out unexpectedly, and she took a deep breath. 'I don't meet many French men who wear berets,' she said. 'The Americans appropriated that fashion.'

'Sibling rivalry, don't you think?'

Carmen tried to imagine how she and Graham looked to the man on the boat as they leaned over the bridge with their shoulders nearly touching but not quite.

Before the dizzy spells started again, she had spent Sundays going for walks in Paris, planning a new route each time to explore the various neighbourhoods. She watched people together, guessing at their relationships, and by studying their body language and how they carried themselves she made up imaginary lives for them. She tried to look into their eyes before they passed her by, hoping to discover something secret about them: an emotional state, an essence. To find out what happiness looked like. To see it reflected in a face. Maybe it would be contagious? But most of the time she caught only irritation or annoyance, and occasionally, when men looked back, flirtation.

Quite often she saw the expressions of dumbstruck awe in tourists who were more interested in manmade structures than in the French people around them. She watched those tourists crane their necks at the Eiffel Tower. Or pose for pictures under the Arc de Triomphe, as tiny dots framed by that overwhelming war memorial. Carmen looked over at Graham, who was staring down at the Seine. 'Do you like asparagus?' she asked.

'No way, I hate it. Why?'

'The French just love asparagus,' she said a little too loudly.

He looked over at her.

'I was just wondering if I remembered little details about you,' she said. The air and open view had improved her mood.

'Well, I remember something about you.'

'Oh, yeah?' she said.

'You were racked by nightmares when we...' he said.

She felt the cold metal railing through her gloves. How, out of their five-year relationship, could he pick such a negative memory and bring it up, taunt her with it? Sure, she'd had nightmares while they were together. She had them before him as well. Did he think he inspired only bad feelings? Behind them, a woman yelled at her son, a little boy dressed in a suit jacket with a bow tie and mini patent shoes. He pulled at his mother's arm, whining to go back, and not forward, across the bridge.

The boy is just like me, she thought, *living for what has passed.*

'I didn't have time for nightmares. If you remember, we didn't sleep all that much,' she said. She had to sit on a bench because her head was whirling. Why was she flirting?

Back then, her parents went out of town most weekends, and she and Graham would spend lazy days in bed with cigarettes and smoke-ring competitions, video marathons of foreign films, takeout food, cocktails and Kama Sutra sex. They threw costume parties for their friends, who would appear as gangsters and molls, movie stars and politicians and ghouls. Some of the themed parties had mysteries to be solved or an ethnic dish to be tested. After graduating from uni, when she and Graham had been broken up for only a couple of months and were not on speaking terms, she confided her travel plans only to her parents and then packed her belongings into boxes in their basement and left the country.

When Carmen got word that he'd followed her to France, she changed her backpacking route to Spain and travelled around the countryside, staying in remote hostels. She stopped checking email altogether, but when she returned to Paris to take up her contract at the school, there were letters waiting – letters asking where she was, telling her he'd have to return to Canada. She had ripped them up and tossed them into the Seine, where pigeons swooped down, expecting her confetti to be food. 'I know what you mean,' she had said aloud to the anxious birds. 'Not very tasty.'

It was only a week ago that she'd answered her cell phone to his baritone voice.

'Your parents,' he admitted. 'I practically had to pay them for your number.' He lived in Amsterdam now and would be in Paris on business. Could they get together for an afternoon?

The rain started again, this time as a fine mist, and the spray crept under her scarf and down her collar. 'I'd better go. I have to teach early tomorrow,' she said.

'It's only five,' he said. But she shrugged and led him to retrace their steps over the Pont Neuf to the Metro station. When he gave her a quick hug goodbye, the handle of the umbrella knocked her in the face. He apologised – for the umbrella or for the relationship, she wasn't sure – but she would surely have a bruise on her cheek.

'It was great to see you again,' he said, his voice seeming a pitch higher.

'You too. It was really great. You haven't changed a bit.'

'Actually, I like to think the last three years have changed me for the better,' he said, and handed her his business card. 'Don't lose it.'

Then she reached for the railing and descended the concrete steps into the deep underground tunnel.

Over the next few weeks, Carmen thought about emailing to thank him for his visit, but she couldn't find the right words, and, anyway, she didn't hear from him, either. One night, when she was getting ready for bed, her best friend, Toni, called from Toronto. This was how she learned that Graham had remained single and the girlfriend he'd told her about at lunch didn't exist. But why would he pretend? Toni suggested he'd wanted to suss her out and see what she had been up to for the time she'd been away, whether she was married and had kids. He wanted to protect himself better this time.

Carmen took the phone and lay on her bed; she watched the Eiffel Tower lights illuminate her room. When Toni asked if she was over him, Carmen sat up and hit her head on the sloping ceiling and screamed.

'Carmen?' Toni said. 'What happened?'

Carmen rubbed her palm into her forehead.

'Are you OK?'

'Yeah, yeah. This stupid *chambre de bonne*. The walls aren't where they're supposed to be.' There was a silence on the line, and Carmen lay back down. 'I'm a bit jumpy right now. I've been having dizzy spells again.'

'I'm sorry. I shouldn't have mentioned Graham.'

'No, it's fine,' she said, and hesitated. 'I'd rather know.'

Somewhere in the building, a child wailed. 'Just a second.' Carmen held the phone against her chest and listened to the little lungs laden with grief or fear or terror, or all three. When he quietened, she went back on the line. 'I'd better go, but thanks for calling. Let's talk again this week.'

'Sure, no problem,' Toni said.

'I appreciate it.'

'Do you?'

'I do.'

'Good, then don't forget I'm here. If you ever want to come home.'

When Carmen hung up, she watched the shifting patterns on her ceiling: diamonds and dots and slashes. Like a flashlight shined into a jewellery box. Her head throbbed as if she'd been drinking; the child started up again, and the sound pierced her thin walls. She closed her eyes, but the spinning in her head got worse and she opened them again. Lying as still as she could on her narrow bed, she took long, deep breaths, one after the other. A stranger – that's what she was here, but Graham had recognised her among these people. He had known her. He knew her still. She didn't belong in this jewellery box. A jagged crystal of light flashed across the ceiling above her and she made a decision: she would not fall. She'd find a ground-floor apartment, even just a room, but with straight walls and curtains that closed at night. It was simple enough but she, Carmen, would stop looking down or backwards. When she stumbled in her dreams – on those Escher-esque stairs – or in her waking life, she would catch herself. Her falling days were over.

Carmen curled into herself and slept a long and dreamless sleep.

PART II

Vancouver (and further afield)

5

Love Bites

Iris Katz's neighbour, Mrs Lowther, returned from six months in Florida to hear suspicious sounds coming through her adjoining wall – incessant scratching, mewing, yowling – and the stench of something rotten. The women didn't know each other except to say hello on the front walk. Two policemen forced their way into Mrs Katz's home but had difficulty getting past the front hall when mewing cats swarmed them. Rottenness blossomed, clinging to their clothes. Officers Jameson and Keele sealed themselves inside the house so that the creatures wouldn't get out. Jameson called out for the 80-year-old resident but there was no answer, only a scattering patter on the linoleum floor and distressed cries. The heat in the place was making the wallpaper peel off and not a single window was open. What they witnessed in the living room made Jameson call an ambulance.

At first, Jameson couldn't understand what he was looking at: a thousand tiny movements in a tower of jumbled animals. The sofa teemed with babies and newborns; live ones with pink noses and suckling mouths. Cats' tails swatted rabbits while rabbits nibbled foam in the furniture or hopped frantically in every direction. Mice scattered under the sofa and one feline surfaced with its jaws clamped on a grey tail flipping wildly. A group of birds, perched on a nearby bookshelf, watched the action below. Jameson thought he saw what looked like a ferret slinking by, but he couldn't tell if the animals splayed out on the floor were even alive. A litter of newborn kittens clumped together by the leg of the couch while their mother stretched out beside them, teats exposed to other creatures that suckled her. There was something else on the sofa, something that confused the men: a large, undulating object. Jameson pushed the couch with his boot and everything alive scampered away.

Then she was revealed. The woman's eyes were closed and her face was cotton white, except for a sprinkling of age spots on her cheeks. Her nightgown, tangled around her legs, was torn up the side and riddled with tiny holes from a nibbling rabbit. Keele gagged when the woman's white hair ruffled up from a tail that whipped out of her bun. In her hairdo was a nest of baby mice.

The odour was urine, excrement and bleach. They held their jackets over their noses but it didn't stop their eyes from watering. 'Oh, Jesus,' Jameson said. He pulled the women's nightgown away from the twitchy rabbit to see fresh spots of blood dotting her legs. When he shook the elderly woman by the shoulder, she didn't respond. Keele backed up and tripped over a cat, before running outside to vomit on the lawn.

Jameson stayed put. 'Ma'am? It's the police.' His voice was muffled from under his jacket. The woman didn't move so he held his breath and leaned in to put a finger on her long and bony wrist. Under the thin blue vein was a slight flutter. *She's got a pulse,* he thought. 'Get back in here, Keele!' he yelled.

The second officer took his time returning and when he did he was plugging his nose with thick fingers.

'My God, would you look at that,' Jameson said. The cats were eating the stuffing from the sofa. 'They're starving.'

Keele averted his eyes to look at the birds on a bookshelf, where one blue and three yellow budgies were preening one another. Then one of the woman's legs slid off the couch and the animals returned to swarm her and Jameson had to shoo them away with his shiny, black boot. Her eyes remained closed and she was so light that Jameson could have been lifting one of his children. He propped her upper body on the armrest. Up close he could see small, red incisions on her neck.

'She's lost a lot of blood, probably over a period of time. We're in the danger zone, Keele. Make the call. Now.'

After the officers checked her in at the hospital, instead of going for their usual drink, they found reasons to part. Jameson didn't mention the case to his wife. They had three young children and as soon as he got home, he took the twins on his lap so she could go to her yoga class.

In his bachelor's apartment, Keele sat on the toilet and wept. He couldn't imagine getting rid of Sherlock, but that night he locked his bedroom door for the first time and his cat whined until four in the morning.

Mrs Iris Katz was treated for 10 mice bites, 58 rabbit bites, 63 scratches and a serious case of toxoplasmosis. The officers questioned her in hospital in the presence of a psychologist, who sat near the door.

'You can't imagine how many homeless cats there are in this city,' Iris told them. 'People go on holidays or move houses and leave them behind.'

Jameson nodded. 'Pets are a big responsibility,' he said.

'You're telling me. Now where are my little babies?' she asked, her blurred eyes searching his. Keele stood slightly behind Jameson and couldn't stop looking at Iris's bandaged neck; then there was her nose, shiny with ointment, and her cheeks were paper white.

'I'm sorry,' Keele said, stepping up to get closer, but before he could continue Jameson cut in. The psychologist typed her notes into a laptop and her tapping annoyed Keele.

'Some will have to be put down because of health problems, and the rest will be treated and put up for adoption,' Jameson said.

'I don't think so,' Iris said.

'No one would be able to manage all that,' Keele said, as he paced the room.

'When my husband was here I managed alright,' she said. 'We looked after them together, and when Henry passed I had my friends. Now they're gone too, just disappeared.' She twisted the hospital sheet in her fingers. 'I'm all that's left.'

Jameson flipped through her file. 'What happened to your brother?'

Iris untwisted the sheet, adjusted her blankets and looked at Keele. 'Did you take the feeding schedule off my fridge, young man? You didn't forget?'

'Mrs Katz, that list was five years old and it only had the names of five pets on it, but you had over a hundred animals, which would be impossible for anyone to manage.'

'How would you know?'

'I have a cat,' Keele said.

She clapped her hands and startled them both. 'What's his name?'

Jameson smiled as Keele leaned in. 'Listen, Mrs Katz, it would have been too much for anyone – that's all I'm saying. We want to help you, do you understand?'

'And I want my babies back. Do you understand that?' she said and pulled her blankets tighter. 'Close the window, I'm cold. Can't you see? I'm cold as ice.'

Officer Keele swiped his hand through his hair and went over to shut the window. The psychologist gestured to Jameson and they huddled over her laptop while Keele went back to her bedside and leaned in. 'We found bites, ma'am, all over your body. They were infected and you needed medical attention.'

'I was only taking a nap,' she said. 'I was resting.'

'Mrs Katz, you were being eaten alive,' he whispered.

Jameson went over to his partner, clamped a hand on his shoulder and asked him to get back to the office; he'd take care of the rest of the interview. Keele didn't look at the woman or acknowledge his partner before leaving the room. When he was gone, Iris turned on her side, putting her back to Jameson.

'It says here in your file that you have a brother.' Jameson tried again. 'Do you? Have any next of kin?'

Iris threw off her covers; she wore a green hospital gown. 'I want to go home now,' she said, dropping one bandaged foot out of the bed.

'That's not possible. You have to stay here until you recover your strength: just a couple more days or so.' Jameson pulled the blankets back over her and she squeezed her eyes shut and fell asleep. The officer listened until her wispy breath become regular, watched her mouth drop open, and then pulled the curtains around her hospital bed closed.

The Katz house was quarantined and her immediate neighbours evacuated, including a displeased Mrs Lowther. Their homes were fumigated while Iris's was gutted. The furniture, infested and multiplying with ticks, mites and cockroaches, was incinerated. Then Iris Katz became a research subject; her health was tracked to see how an 80-year-old coped with such a variety of bacteria in her body.

Iris was summoned to court and had to testify for reasons of insurance. With no legal guardian or living family members, the Public Guardian and Trustee were notified and she was assessed as to whether she was liable for damages to her neighbour's property.

In court, Iris explained to the judge: 'I walked by Bowsers Pet Shop every day and since I had mice eating at my dried food, I thought a cat was a good idea. But a cat alone is not a happy critter; they need company like us humans. So I got two.'

The judge nodded. 'They certainly liked each other better than you could have imagined.'

'They caught mice together; they were a good team.' Then she had a coughing attack and an assistant poured her a cup of water. 'I found strays on the street. All the time. I couldn't just leave them there, could I?' She looked up into the judge's eyes. 'We have a duty to our living creatures.' Her coughing started up again so he took an adjournment and Mrs Katz followed her lawyer out of the courtroom, asking him if he had any pets; he didn't.

Back on the stand, Iris looked around the room, catching Jameson's eye, before answering. 'I don't know how they multiplied so quickly. I only had two of each to start.'

Jameson and Keele were in the front row and Jameson leaned over. 'Like in Noah's ark?' he whispered, but Keele was playing with his cell phone in his lap and didn't acknowledge his partner.

'When did you get your first pet, Mrs Katz?' the judge asked.

Iris twirled a strand of thin white hair around her fingers and looked up at the ceiling. 'Yesterday? Oh no, just a minute. My birthday was last week, I turned seventy-five. The cats were a gift: that's right.'

'Mrs Katz?' the judge said.

'A gift from…?'

'Mrs Katz?'

'Yes, your honour.'

'You swore on the Bible, did you not?'

She nodded and then told the court how she'd been dreaming about her husband when it happened, how he used to tuck her in at night before getting in on his side. He'd smooth her hair back and give her little kisses on her face until she was covered in tiny, wet spots, which air-dried before she fell asleep. Her creatures reminded her of his preening.

'I was drinking my tea, like on any other afternoon but I felt so tired that I didn't make it to my bedroom. I love them all, you know; they weren't a burden.'

Iris was kept in the hospital for two weeks before being transferred to a seniors' care centre. She had no choice. She was considered a danger to herself and made a ward of the state.

A nurse led her into her new room at the home, which was only five blocks away from her own house.

'There isn't enough space here for my creatures,' she said, eyeing the single bed in the single room.

'We'll take good care of you,' the nurse said.

'And what do you think I've been doing with myself for seventy-five years?' Iris scratched at her bandages.

'Eighty. You're eighty now,' the nurse said, pulling her hands away from her wounds. 'And we don't allow pets in the facility.'

'Then get me out of here.'

'Iris, it's going to be OK.'

'Mrs Katz,' she said, turning away from the nurse. 'If you don't mind.'

The nurse opened the dresser drawer to check that it had been cleaned out from the previous patient. She ran her finger along the windowsill and wrinkled her nose at the trace of dust.

'There are lots of fun activities here, and you'll make fast friends. We'll keep you real busy.' She patted her patient on the back and left the room, but Iris was opening the small window overlooking the street and didn't hear the nurse leave.

'My brother died five years ago. He was never married. Todd never met a woman he could love. He helped me take care of my family and had dinner with Henry and me every weekend. If he didn't eat with us… well, I just don't know. You see, normally my brother survived on liquids. On alcohol, to be plain and clear.'

She was only 10 when she discovered one of her brother's secrets: Todd would burn ants with a magnifying glass, cut worms into little segments and pull the arms off starfish. Iris pretended she didn't have a brother. Running to her parents never helped, nor did throwing temper tantrums. Instead, she became a saviour of creatures, stealing them from Todd's fish tank, which he'd fill with sand and bits of grass after mowing the lawn. He kept a black spider, some garden snakes and a white mouse. Iris took the mouse from the dirty aquarium, put the wriggling thing into a paper bag and released it in the forest.

Behind the seniors' home was a grassy park where she was allowed to go for walks alone. That afternoon, she lay down in the grass and napped. When she awoke her hair was tangled up with purple clovers. She looked in the tall grass for living things and thought of Todd, who had, years after his boyhood experiments, become a biologist. Iris collected insects and put them in her pocket or held them loosely in her palm to smuggle them into her room. When she asked the kitchen staff for a container for her 'rock collection' the cook gave her a big empty jam jar. Now she held a microcosm of life in her hands – from the smallest red ants, to centipedes, grasshoppers, a ladybug, a pink garden worm and a spider. She named the spider Todd and the candy-red ladybug, with four spots, after herself. Then came another jar, and the week after, another.

Iris filled each one with creatures, gave them beds of grass, weeds and flower petals and poked air holes in the lid. Her collection lived under her single bed at the seniors' home, and at night she couldn't sleep for the excitement of the life underneath her, pulsating with promise.

6

Candyman

He's flat on his back, crushing a patch of wet grass. We circle him, watching his lips sputter out bubbles of saliva. His mouth curls to kiss the air. I stare at the wrinkles carved into his cheeks like the map of rivers we study in geography class. How can anyone be that old? We've been standing here all recess watching him shake. First his arm reaches to grab the grass and then his head rolls from side to side as if he's saying 'no' to someone.

'Mr Candyman?' I whisper and the kids look up to me. It's like we're watching a car crash, where we can't look away but don't know what else to do. There's little Susie, who calls the old guy grandpa because she doesn't know any better, and Peter, who is slow in the head, standing there with his finger up his nose. My friend Benny leans against me taking deep breaths and even his eyes are glued to the old man, whose feet are jerking up and down on the grass. This is the first time any of us has seen the Candyman outside, and he looks much bigger in real life.

'Mr Candyman?' I want to go up and smell him, I mean really whiff his face, and touch his mop hair. I want to see his eyes up close, not through some dusty pane of glass into the shadowy basement room where he lives. But his eyelids are squeezed shut like he'd been real scared before falling down. Is he dying? I saw him two days ago and he didn't look too good. To get to his place the kids sneak out of the schoolyard, crawl through the prickly bushes and run across Manitoba Street to the grey stucco house, number 14. At the back there's an old kitchen window, and at the bottom of the wooden frame three little holes – for air to come in or to put birdseed out, who knows? We heard about him from the older kids about a month ago. That he would give us free candy through his basement window but if we left our fingers too long in the holes he would chop them off. That last time he was shaking as he put a gold-wrapped fudge swirl into one of the holes. 'Push it further out, Mister,' I called.

He looked at me through the window with his yellowy eyes. He never put a candy on our side of the ledge but made us stick our fingers into the air hole to get it. All the kids stood back except for Susie, who has the longest hair you've ever seen. She hid behind me and covered her eyes with her hair. Well, we never knew what the Candyman would do to us, did we? That's why none of us would tell our moms about him. We only heard him speak once and that's when he whispered through the window to Harry Winters, a quiet kid in grade five, who never went back again. When we grilled Harry, he just shook his head no, and no it was; he never told us what was said. Did he ever tell his parents? I mean is it right for a little kid with a harelip and shy eyes to go around his whole life with the Candyman's secret filling his head?

The old man looks like a bum now, lying on the wet grass, with his dirty fingernails that need a good cutting, that's for sure. Doesn't he have a wife to take care of him? There's a bad smell coming from the dark spot on his pants. Around his private parts. And he's shaking just like my dad when he drinks too much. My mom kicked my dad out of the house and yelled at him that as far as she was concerned he had a life detention. Then she warned me not to get myself into hot water like him.

It's cold on the grassy hill outside our school, and I'm shivering because I forgot to take my parka even after mom told me to. I wonder if the Candyman is cold in his short-sleeved shirt? Maybe he's just having a bad dream, his leg shaking like a crazy dog. Benny whispers that Mrs Tate, our home-class teacher, is coming out of the schoolyard and walking over to us. We're not allowed to leave the school grounds but she'll forget when she sees what we're looking at. It'll take her at least a minute to get to us so I stick a candy into my mouth before recess is over and you have to spit your gum out in the garbage at the school entrance. It's caramel crunch – my favourite – which melts in my mouth until I get to the nut in the centre. I ate about six of those already and on good days I knew he'd give me two candies. Now that the old guy is being taken away I wonder what will happen to all his sweets. I know from experience that candies go bad if no one's around to give them out. Once my dad hid my Halloween stash and I found it just before Christmas in the cupboard beside the stove with his empty beer cans, all gooey and stuck together.

The ambulance's siren cries and the recess bell rings over and over again. Benny is taking bigger and bigger breaths, and I have an ache in my head the size of a football. Then there she is: Mrs Tate. She stares at me with her huge owl eyes behind round glasses. She looks like she can see right through me to all the bad things I've done.

'Back to the yard, everyone. You know better than to leave the school grounds.' She rounds us up. 'Recess is over. Leave the man to the doctors, there's nothing we can do.'

'But Mrs Tate—' I say and she gives me *the look* so I shut up. It takes a good while for her to get a crowd of staring kids away from a man lying on a grassy hill face up to the sky with his eyes squeezed shut and his pant leg wet from pee.

In class she calls on me. 'Timothy, I want you to read the next page of *A Wrinkle in Time* and speak up.'

Her eyes are like Luke Skywalker's lightsabre lasering into me. I look down at my pencil and finish scratching off the gold H in the letters Berol HB. I can't answer her because there's a frog stuck in my throat.

After school I go straight home to my room and take out all the candy wrappers I saved, smooth them out, and look at the rainbow of colours together. Golden caramel, red cherry, green mint, brown chocolate and yellow lemon. I imagine eating them all at once and wonder what flavour it'd be, so I smell all the wrappers at the same time. Then I put them back between the pages of my *X-Men* and hide it at the bottom of the bookshelf.

It's been seven days since the ambulance took the man away. I know cause I made marks in my calendar and went to his kitchen window every day. Mostly when I peer in all I see are shadows. But today there's something moving in there. Yes, it's definitely moving. It's black and white and pawing its way around the corner, playing with the dust. I tap on the window and he looks up at me, does a sideways jump and bounces out of my sight.

'Here, kitty, kitty. Psst. Hey, little guy.'

Nothing moves for about five whole minutes then I hear the school bell ringing.

The next day, I bring the get-well card I made in art class – it's got a big candy cane, the biggest ever. Creeping around the side of the grey house, I step over weeds and kick at some wet newspapers. There's a basement door with a window and a mail slot in it. I knock and wait with one foot on the path ready to run. No answer. I try the glass window: *tap tap*, and hear the cat cry. I open the mailbox and peer in. The kitty is sitting there looking at me so I drop my card through the slot and watch him run up to it and paw it around the floor. Then I get on my bike and go home.

'Eat your dinner instead of playing with it,' my mom says.

I want to tell her about the cat but her eyes have that blurry look. I always know when I get back from school if she's in her bedroom watching her soaps or at the table drinking coffee until she gets really hyper and cleans the house from top to bottom and I have to stay in my room till she's finished.

The next morning at recess I sneak across the street to the side of the stuccoed house, running my hand along the rough wall and pulling off bits of grey rocks. I don't tell anyone I still visit the Candyman because they'd think I'm dumb. The other kids have already given up on him. I put my nose against his dark window and through the holes smell dust and cat pee. There's nothing to do but sit down on the brown grass in the backyard and wait. The black-and-white cat comes into the kitchen and jumps onto the other side of the windowsill.

'Hi, furball!' I stroke his neck through the candy holes in the windowsill and accidentally push him off the ledge. He hops back up and purrs at me. I take out the milk carton from my lunch bag and pour a few drops onto my finger and stick it through the hole. His sandpaper tongue licks my finger clean and I pour more milk through the hole in the window so it splashes onto the ledge and down the wall. I can tell the cat likes me very much.

The next day in class when I have a lot to think about, Mrs Tate bugs me.

'Timothy, tell the class what Christopher Columbus was searching for on his famous expedition.'

Every day she asks more and more questions, like I'm a criminal under a spotlight. 'Timothy, did you read the discovery chapter?'

My Berol pencil is so small that I can barely hold on to it. That afternoon I think about finally telling Mom about the old man and maybe she can call the cemeteries to see if he died or something. Before going home, I walk over to the house and for the first time ever go right up the front steps and ring the doorbell. A man with a shiny head opens the door and stares at me and I think maybe he's the Candyman's roommate.

'What are you selling?' he asks, ''cause I don't want any.'

My hands are sticky in my pockets and I hold onto my pet rock, turning it over and over.

'Um, I was just wondering if, if, you know the—.'

The phone rings and he turns away, leaving the door open, so I step into his living room and see a TV bigger than I've ever seen in my life. I hear his voice all mean on the phone and turn around and run back to my house and to my room with the door closed and no appetite for dinner.

By Sunday it's been almost two weeks since we've seen the old man on the grassy hill and I am ready to give up my detective work. I just have one question for the bald guy so I ride my bike to the house for the last time. I have so much homework to do now, like write a book report and do five pages of math. As I round the corner I almost run over a pigeon, who loses a couple of feathers. Turning onto Manitoba Street I can't believe what I see. There, right in the front yard, is Mr Candyman himself. He's in a blue-and-red lawn chair with a baby's bib on and a nurse is feeding him something from a bowl. I'm about to get out of there when she calls out. 'Hello, young man. Do you live around here?'

I nod.

'Well, that's good news. Do you know Mr Treat, then?'

My head is getting real hot. 'Um, I, I'm not sure. ma'am.'

Very slowly, the Candyman moves his head up and down. He smiles at me a little and reaches his hand out and I don't know what to do so I get on my bike and ride away as fast as I can, knocking over a garbage can in my way. When I get to Benny's house I bang on his bedroom window and wave at him to follow me.

The nurse grins when she sees us ride up.

'Well, hello again! Mr Treat, now you have two visitors.' She laughs in this soft way and because Benny's with me and she's a nurse, I feel OK. Just then the mean man from upstairs comes out of his door and onto the porch and stands there, looking at us.

'Nigel, could you get your father some water?' the nurse says, and the mean man gets a cup of water for the old guy. Then the nurse looks at us.

'Would you two boys help me with something? Mr Treat has diabetes and isn't allowed to eat sweets.'

Jonathan, the used-to-be-mean-man, shakes his head and pats the Candyman on his white mop hair and goes back into the house. Ben and I look at each other.

'We found two boxes of candy in his apartment and there's absolutely no way he's going to be eating them. Are you Mr Treat?'

Mr Treat looks at us. His eyes water and his hands shake like two leaves in the wind. He starts coughing pretty hard and the nurse lady pats him on the back and gives him some water. I take a candy from his warm, leathery hand.

7

If You Had to Lose

Her leg reappeared in dreams: floating down in a parachute, being swept in by the tide; once it was wrapped like a birthday present in a long, thin box tied up with a yellow satin ribbon.

When she was 10 and had sleepovers by candlelight, her friends would ask each other the following questions:

> If you could save only one person from a fire, would it be your mom or your dad?
>
> Who do you love best: your dog or the answer to question 1?
>
> If a crazy psycho had a knife and was going to chop off one part of your body but not kill you, which part would you lose?

For Marie it was always a toe, and when her friends asked for something bigger she said her hair because it was already dead. Her long, silky red hair was the kind you see in shampoo ads for Pantene Plus or John Frieda's anti-frizz. Her best friend since childhood, Patty, had the *before hair* you see in that same ad; a frizzy mess taking up so much of the page that it floated out of the edges of the magazine. Poor Patty. She got headaches trying to brush out all those tangles.

Marie was now 15 and had been off grade 10 for a month since the accident. Two weeks were spent in the hospital and then two weeks at home. All the get-well cards had come in; her boyfriend, Miles, had visited with flowers; the school journalist had interviewed her; and her teachers had been calling her mom weekly to check up on her. Up until last week, when a girl in grade eight was abducted, and Marie's 15 minutes of fame were over. Everyone forgot about her except Patty, who still brought over homework and the daily gossip: like how a new girl in class was sitting in Marie's seat, how their biology teacher smelled like dog shit and how their arch-enemy Janice lost her virginity on a dare. Patty tried to make Marie sound cool: 'You're like a superhero with a magical leg.' Only Marie didn't believe in that shit.

What kept her busy while in recovery – at least for a little while – were crosswords, sudoku, glossy magazines, even a teach-yourself-knitting kit. But Marie chewed on the yarn until it was soggy and then threw it up to the ceiling like cooked pasta, aiming to make it stick, but it never did. She was so bored she begged her mom for more candy, music, magazines – although she defaced all of those wide-smiling, two-legged models – and to top up her pay-as-you-go cell phone, which was her lifeline to the outside world. But often her old phone didn't hold charge, or her friends were in class and couldn't talk. Sometimes at lunch they'd text back, but mostly her mother and her brother were her daily companions.

Will always came home after school stomping and slamming some door or other and pretending not to hear Marie calling from her bed until Mom ordered him into his sister's room. He always looked as if he'd forgotten what had happened to his sister until he saw her in bed. Will was 12 and smelled like salt-and-vinegar chips and had greasy fingers. Marie would usually ask for a popsicle or a cookie or something sweet to get her out of her *poor me* mood, but she was gaining weight lying in bed for so much of the day and shouldn't eat as many calories as she used to. She was so bored she fantasised about slashing her wrists with the nail scissors and leaving her blood all over the place, making her brother cry for a change. But then her mom would lose her apartment deposit from the mess and they would have to move.

It was post-traumatic stress she was dealing with, according to the therapist who came in to talk to her once a week. First was the shock of the accident and then two weeks in the hospital eating soup and mush and then daily rehab treatments and always the fear of the doctor deciding she'd have to lose even more of her leg. The therapist assured her she'd get through it, though, and as luck had it, the rest of her leg, including the knee, would stay with her. In the hospital, they measured her for a prosthetic. Every day they came in to measure and try the fit. It exhausted her and near the end of her stay she caught the flu and they sent her home to recover; her body too weak to withstand other germs.

'I know this is very difficult for you,' her mother said while stroking her back, 'but the prosthetic will cost us six thousand dollars, and if you want to walk again, you'll have to learn to love the thing.'

That's what they'd started calling it: *the thing*. They didn't have insurance because her mom couldn't afford it and now she had to pay out of her own pocket because Marie had ignored the 'keep out' sign. There was a chance that the medical services plan would assist them since her mom was single and financially struggling, but they were waiting to hear back.

Marie knew that she wasn't supposed to cut through the abandoned construction yard to get to school. Everyone knew that but did it anyway, and then came a sudden storm that shifted the concrete blocks, one of which came loose and fell from such a height, catching her on the leg.

She felt like a prisoner at home while she lay in bed healing, waiting for her mom to get her more library books after she finished all of *Twilight* and *Harry Potter* (which she wouldn't have been caught dead with at school). Also, her TV time had been limited.

'Only three hours a day, young lady,' her mother said. 'Don't force me to take the idiot box out of your room.'

Marie was pretty sure her mom kept her ear to the door when she was glued to *The Simpsons* or a soap opera. Trying to imitate one of the actresses on *One Life to Live* she would cry out so that her mother, her brother, or the neighbours – someone, anyone – would hear: 'Oh Joey, how could you? I loved you more than she ever will!' But no one came running in. Her mom was moody and tired now that she had to work double shifts to pay for the accident as well as maybe even take out a loan.

Still, Marie pushed her buttons by calling out for something when she knew her mom was late for work. One morning she pushed her too far and broke through her mother's patience. She screamed with a mouth so wide Marie could see her tonsils. *She was so goddamn fed up. She couldn't do everything. What was she: a full-time servant?* But as soon as she finished the rant there came an open-mouthed silence from her daughter and mom jumped into her bed and hugged her, saying over and over how sorry she was for her poor, dear child. Mom curled up next to her and Marie wet her shoulder with tears, tears that sprang out of her like little bombs, like her brother's spit bombs made of paper chewed to pulp and shot out of a straw. Her mother soothed her by patting her head as if she were a pet and making her hair lay flat and ugly. Then mom inhaled sharply when she saw the time and leapt up to go to work. Pronto. Marie knew that her mother had missed her own lunch due to Marie's neediness and she spent the afternoon alone with acidic guilt swirling in her guts, hobbling on crutches to the toilet to wash the tears from her face. Later though, when she had calmed down and lay back in bed, she held on to her stump and it was warm and vibrating with energy. She could almost see the rest of her leg as it used to be, her pink polished toes winking at her.

Most days, though, she lay in bed counting the dots in the ceiling tiles – like the ones you see in dentist's offices. There were 25 dots across and 25 dots down and if she did the math right she could figure out the whole square. Then the next until she had nearly finished calculating the whole ceiling; the tricky part was the half tiles at the walls. Still, the hours in her bedroom dragged while the days melded into two weeks of purgatory. Whenever she dozed in the daytime, the meds made her dreams wild and disturbed and a few times she woke up screaming because of dark objects dropping from the sky, through her ceiling and onto her bedspread. In one dream it was her own amputated leg falling. She was never fast enough to catch or avoid these objects and as the dream repeated in variations they became heavier: a fridge, a boat and then a house. When she woke it was in a sweat and she was never sure what day of the week it was. Admitting this to the therapist meant she learned it was part of the grieving process and that the dreams would eventually subside.

On Valentine's Day, Patty delivered a card from Marie's boyfriend,

Miles, who had soccer practice and said he couldn't make it over after. He'd signed off with 'luv', which made her cry and made Patty squirm since Patty hadn't got a single card on the day of love. Patty asked to see Marie's leg and Marie quickly lifted her blankets and pulled off the gauze and watched her friend's face drop at the shiny pink stump peeping out. Then Marie grabbed Patty's hand and forced her to touch the bumpy part and Patty yelped, then laughed, then had to lie down. Marie's mother brought her a glass of water. At least now Patty knew for sure and could tell people at school that Marie wasn't lying or being Miss Dramatic or something.

Will came in one afternoon with a magazine article and, since she was sleeping, left it on her bed with a big happy face drawn on it. It showed an American athlete, model and activist named Aimee Mullins, who was born with missing fibula bones and had to have her legs amputated as a baby. Marie admired the woman's blond hair and was shaken up by the unexpected look of determination in her eyes. The next day, Will brought in a printout of the same girl dressed up to look like a cheetah. 'See? See?' he said. 'It's so cool – look at how real that is. And you could be the panther girl,' he said. 'Or a lioness.'

Another time he came running too fast into her room and smashed his shin on her bed frame. He jumped around in pain, screaming something, and it took her a moment to hear the words: 'Blade Runner! Blade Runner!' as he thrust out a photo of a South African athlete who had blades for feet. Then Will limped out of her room and she grieved at his cries of pain. If only she could feel that pain again. The stories interested her for a brief time but they didn't have internet at home and she couldn't find out more. Plus, the idea of running before she could walk was so far from her reality that she slipped the articles under her bed and forgot about them.

When her mother came in later with a tray of tomato soup and orange juice and her favourite Ritz crackers, Marie didn't look up. She wanted to punish her mom – like it was her fault she was lying here in this bed. Well, it was her mom's decision to have her and all. It did mean her mom had chosen to put her into this world, and then the world chose to lose her leg. Imagine if it had been something else, like her brain, heart or eyes. The thought made her want to throw up and she pushed away the soup bowl.

If you had to choose, what could you live without?

It could have been worse, but it made Marie angry to be told that, to be told she was lucky. She would never dance again or do gymnastics or learn to ride a horse. She would always have to take off her appendage before she got into bed with someone. If she ever got married, she'd have to find someone who didn't mind having a one-legged wife; Paul McCartney hadn't minded. Or had he?

On that subject, Will told her not to worry, because Aimee Mullins had just gotten married and so she could too.

'Who?' she'd asked.

He pulled out the dusty articles from under her bed. 'The cheetah girl.'

She reread them and felt something inside her shift. From now on, though, she would always, for the rest of her life, have to explain to anyone who asked, what had happened. The therapist was helping her to create a story out of it, one that could be repeated without flinching. *Her* story. The story of what was missing and what was dearly missed.

The fact that Miles hadn't visited in so long, that Patty wasn't coming over every day after school now and that her teachers rarely sent feedback on her homework set her adrift. Her friends were leaving her, but the memory of her leg would not let her be.

In the third week since she left the hospital, just when it seemed Marie had lost her mind, her amputation wound healed over and the doctor came over to show her how to put on the new carbon-fibre prosthetic. She learned how to secure it, but the gel pad between her stump and the leg didn't feel stable. It was like a whole week had gone by and that's all she could focus on: balancing on the crutches, doing muscle-strengthening exercises in her upper arms and left leg, learning how to be her new self. It all made her so tired. Her muscles needed her help, the doctor said. With a rehabilitation therapist she was kept busy daily and so there was no time to see Patty and she missed out on a week of homework. When the weekend came, and with it, Patty, Marie understood how much she had missed.

For the first time in their friendship Patty had a boyfriend.

'You mean Josh? *That* Josh?' She kept her voice even.

While Patty painted Marie's fingernails in Luscious Lavender, she explained, in excruciating detail, how at the bus stop on Monday, Josh smiled at her and then started talking to her. They found out they had both applied to the same college and before he got off the bus, he wrote down his phone number on the palm of her hand. Josh, with his blue and silver rugby jacket, spiky blond hair, and nearly black eyes. Marie had to admit that Patty had done something to herself: even her hair was straightened and shinier than Marie's. Now her pastel make-up was perfectly applied because she was taking a modelling course at Blanche MacDonald's. Patty had such nice eyelashes, long and curled-up, while Marie hadn't even bothered to put on mascara for her friend's visit.

'Now we both have a guy,' she told Marie and blew on her wet nails. 'Me and Josh and you and Miles can hang out once you're back on your feet.' She blushed. 'Sorry. I didn't mean that.'

There was a pause. 'Yeah, sure. Sounds like a plan.'

Patty rushed over to the dresser mirror and reapplied her lip gloss. 'When are you getting out of this hell hole?' she said, as she pulled her jacket on and hardly turned to wave goodbye.

So is this what it was like to have friends after all? First betrayed by Miles, who'd only come to see her once in two weeks. Abandoned shortly after by Patty, but then Patty only reminded her of regrets now, like how it was supposed to be her dumping Miles for Josh when the school dance came up. Like how Marie had planned it all out and now Patty had messed up her plan. Like how annoying that was.

That evening she called Miles and made him promise to come over after school the next day and see her. And he did. But without a kiss and hardly a look into her eyes, because he was studying her prosthetic.

'You can always hit an attacker over the head with it,' Miles said, bench-pressing her appendage to the ceiling, up and down. She sprawled across her bed, watching him swing the leg like a baseball bat.

'You could crack a guy's skull with it too,' he said.

'Yeah, right.'

'Or…?' His eyes narrowed, thinking.

'Or you could try walking with it,' she snapped. 'It cost six thousand dollars.'

He aimed it at her like a rifle as if to blow her head off but she didn't react. Then he blew apart her bedroom wall. She grabbed for it and he pinned her down, trying finally to kiss her, but she turned away before he could. She could no longer storm out the way she used to because it took time to put her leg on and find the crutches. When he left, she beat up her pillow.

That evening, she leaned over her second-floor bedroom windowsill and, hurling the leg out, aimed for the creek below their house. Instead, it bounced off the maple tree, fell rustling through its dry branches and landed on the lawn. For a moment, Marie wondered how many ants she had crushed, but the thing had itched like hell and she didn't feel like it was the right size. Immediately, though, she regretted it, thinking of how her mother's face would boil when she told her.

A deep sleep overtook Marie and when she awoke in the morning, she felt buoyed and free. She breathed in and forgot, for a moment, what was missing; she forgot about the accident until she saw the wheelchair in her room and felt something heavy, wrapped in a towel lying on the bed beside her. Before she could understand what had happened, Will came hurtling in before school and told her he wouldn't tell Mom, but she was lucky he had found it before it got rained on. He stood there waiting for his sister to thank him so she gave him a quick hug and the 10 dollars in her wallet, which made him smile like a monkey. What was the use of money anymore?

Now she understood that she *was* lucky. It wasn't as if she'd been chosen by some deity or something, but that she, based on her own instincts, had stopped in the construction yard, at the right moment and because of it, saved her head. The concrete block would have emptied her brain of memories, cleaned her out like a shiny, silver teapot – all the beauty in her world would have seeped out onto the pavement, like sugary syrup.

Her doctor told her it would take some time until she got used to her new leg and that her mind might rebel, pretending the prosthetic didn't belong, rejecting it: the way Marie felt about her friends. But the doctor said she had to be patient, speak to her therapist regularly, and practise using it every day so that, slowly, her body would learn to lean on it, to *befriend* the leg.

She wondered where the remains of her body part went. She had signed a consent form that her limb could be used for research, but she had asked the doctor not to tell her how it could be used and for what. The mystery of not knowing was easier to accept than the finality of her own flesh being discarded. But then again, she always wondered. Maybe her toes were donated to lepers? Or her shin bone was a replacement for someone in need? Could all body parts be recycled? She missed her leg more than she missed Miles's brown eyes. No loss would be greater than the disappearance of her five rose-painted toes. She thought about the questions her 10-year-old friends had asked themselves at sleepovers: *what would you lose if you had to lose?* And she remembered that she'd offered one toe and not five. Her anger stayed with her in the daytime as she stared at what was missing – the absence of her leg against the sheet on her bed. At night, though, she had dreams where she was running with her new leg, racing against Aimee Mullins on a never-ending track. They were both dressed up – she as the panther overtaking the great cheetah.

And then Marie was running so fast that, all at once, she launched into flight.

8

His Golden Woman

To my grandmother, Sarah

Smoke plumed out of the skyscraper and little figures fell from the building. Millie rubbed her eyes and looked again, deciding it was pieces of the building dropping off, but when she squinted, it looked a lot like people. She reclined in her La-Z-Boy and the tips of her slippered feet touched the dusty screen. It reminded her of *The Towering Inferno*, a film that had given her more than one nightmare over the years. Since Millie had the power to mute the noise and stop the images, she did so. The world, from inside her bedroom, was still in her hands.

On her night table were four plastic cups of prune purée, the colour of muddy water. She was late taking her medications and found it more difficult to keep up with the nurses' demands. Millie swallowed the six pills with some orange juice, but couldn't make herself eat the purée so she tossed the cups one by one into the garbage can and threw a newspaper on top to hide the evidence.

The smoke that came out of that tall building on the TV must have been a cataract clouding her vision. She would ask the nurse to make an appointment with the eye doctor, the handsome one. What was the point in having good eyesight unless there was something pleasant to look at?

All morning the image stayed in her mind: little slivers falling off the building and onto the pavement. Would the people below have time to escape? It must have been a remake of that horrible film and she wondered why the Hollywood studios didn't come up with new ideas. That Jewish director – what was his name? – had rejected her life story for one of his films. Imagine, it had cost her five dollars to send the manuscript from Vancouver to Hollywood and all she got back was a form letter. The worst part was that he went ahead and made her story without her and the film won an Academy Award. He stole her ideas without paying for them, or giving her credit. She could have given him advice on how to dramatise the scene in the work camp and the escape through underground tunnels, if only he had answered her phone calls. Since receiving his letter, she refused to watch any films on TV and warned her son, daughter-in-law and grandchildren to do the same.

Millie opened her faux wood dresser drawer and pulled out a cookie tin, camouflaged under her underwear. Inside was a handkerchief tied up with ribbon, from which she removed an amber necklace – the cool stone as large as her palm. When she held the jewel up to the window, she admired the cloudy, green amber with bits of fossilised nature sealed inside. She slipped the necklace into her pocket, put the tin back and slammed the drawer shut. Her hands shook as she smoothed the bedspread on either side of her and pursed her mouth at thoughts that flashed like electric currents through her brain. Millie's stomach growled. The clock read 11.35am, which was nearly time for lunch, so she decided to stroll down to the foyer and say hello to her friends the parakeets.

In the hall, she met up with Yvette, who had refused to wash her hair for a week; the nurses who tried to get her out of her wheelchair and into the shower would get a bite or kick. When Millie sneezed, it nearly knocked Yvette to the floor.

'I'll huff and I'll puff and I'll blow your house down!' Millie sang, pulling bits of fluff out of her friend's hair.

Yvette held a necklace Millie had given her the day before. 'I've never had anything so shiny,' she said, looking up at Millie with radiant eyes and an appreciation that Millie hadn't seen since her husband abandoned the world. Millie pushed Yvette's wheelchair to the elevator.

'Speed up,' Yvette commanded.

'I am.'

'Not fast enough.' They just missed running over the new nurse's toes. 'Better luck next time,' Yvette said.

'Good morning, ladies,' said the nurse.

'Good afternoon,' said Millie.

'Why are you in such a rush?' The nurse leaned down to Yvette. 'Lunch isn't on yet.'

'You must be the new one,' Yvette said.

'I started on Monday. I'm Jemmy.'

'Jenny,' Millie repeated.

'Jemmy, with two m's. It's Filipino.'

'Let me ask you this, Jemmy: what day is it today?'

The nurse hesitated. 'Thursday.'

'That's right, and Thursday is a special day at Riverbanks.'

'What's special about it?' Jemmy smiled.

Millie and Yvette looked at each other and Jemmy crossed her arms over her starched uniform. 'Well?'

'Thursday is Jell-O day,' Yvette announced. 'And Jell-O day is sacred around here.'

The dining room, decorated in shades of brown and orange, seemed unchanged since the '70s. Back then, some of those now at Riverbanks in the east end of Vancouver were out on the streets, protesting the Vietnam War or converting to vegetarianism. Others were housewives and competed in baking competitions, and cooked hams and turkeys for family dinners, passing down favourite recipes from grandmothers to mothers, daughters, nieces, aunts and cousins.

Now where were they? Eating unrecognisable slop out of plastic bowls. The food at Riverbanks came in shades of grey, white and brown. Mystery meat swam in grey gravy. White potato salad was bathed in mayonnaise. Vegetables were cooked until they fell apart. They were served a variety of soft foods that slid easily down the throat.

Millie sat at a table with Yvette, Herman and Dorothy, and when Jemmy strode over, Millie covered her sandwich with the palm of her hand.

Jemmy said, 'You'd better finish your lunch or you won't get you-know-what, Mrs Borkowski.'

'That's a threat,' Yvette murmured, pushing chunks of banana and canned mandarins around her plate. A fruit plate was the alternative meal choice.

Millie's hands shook as she picked up her sandwich. Blanched iceberg lettuce wilted out the side and the egg filling was the same colour as the bread.

'They only make Jell-O once a week,' Yvette said to Millie.

'I know. You don't need to tell me.' The sandwich disintegrated in Millie's fingers.

'Here, use your knife and fork if it's not cooperating,' Jemmy said, still hovering by their table.

Herman laughed, which made him choke. The nurse fed him water and kept watch over Millie, who'd encircled her plate of mushy egg sandwich with her arms, like a fortification. Dorothy and Herman ate their sandwiches with knives and forks.

'When you finish yours, will you help me out?' Millie asked Herman who chomped down on his fork, dentures hitting metal.

'Anything for you, lovely,' he said, pushing his teeth back into his mouth. Dorothy poked him with a bony finger and glared at Millie.

The moment everyone was waiting for came, and bowls of Jell-O were set down so hard they jiggled like cellulite. Dorothy stuck her finger into the centre of her bowl to break up the plastic surface. Millie stabbed hers three times with a spoon and brought the bowl up to her lips to drink. Some of the gelatine bounced down her blouse and into her lap.

For a few moments, the world was in its rightful place. Men and women flirted, pursing stained lips. Jell-O: ah, and red at that, the colour of cherries and passion, blood and sex. It reminded Millie of sucking back oysters with her late husband at a beachside restaurant.

Yvette tried to collect their bowls in order to catch the busboy's attention. At that moment, Dorothy cried, 'The ring! The ring on her finger! Look!' and lunged for Yvette's hand. 'That's mine! That was for me! She stole it! She took it right off my hand, while I was sleeping! It was a gift!'

Yvette tucked her hands up under her armpits and looked out the window. The residents watched Dorothy's face turn pink, red and then deep mauve. The nurses gathered around to soothe her, but Dorothy was on a rampage. 'My diamond – that's my diamond! Tell her to give it back. She – she's a thief! She went into my – she broke into my room!'

The accused Yvette kept her eyes lowered because, although she hadn't stolen it, it was given to her with a promise not to tell. A nurse called the front desk for medication and everyone turned to watch as Dorothy hyperventilated, slipped out of the nurse's grasp and passed out on the floor. Millie watched the handsome male nurse, who looked like a movie star from California, bend over her. His long, blonde hair covered his face but she could imagine his full mouth planted on her own to give her mouth-to-mouth resuscitation.

'Ungrateful wretch. Look at her, getting kisses from the nurse,' Millie told Yvette. 'When she acts like a child, she should be scolded, not rewarded.' Millie's stomach soured, the effects of Jell-O curdling with coffee, and she escaped the dining room frenzy.

The walls of the lounge were floral: pansies and roses intertwined on a gable, and yellow lamps dangled from the ceiling. Three people huddled together on an orangey-brown sofa: Marty, a former mathematics professor, then Ivan and his girlfriend, Nancy. They sat side-by-side, staring ahead like birds on a wire. Marty mumbled and Ivan shifted closer to Nancy.

'What do you got in your pockets, Marty? Are you stealing cookies from the kitchen again?' Ivan said and squeezed Nancy's hand. She squeezed back.

'Two times two is 43.' Marty looked to Ivan for a response.

'No. No, that doesn't seem right.' Ivan held his hands out and lifted two fingers on each hand. 'Count these.'

The mathematician looked at Ivan's fingers, grunted and peeled himself off the plastic couch.

'Marty, wait, come back and I'll show you!' Ivan shouted, but Marty was gone. 'What can you do but help the man?' he told his girlfriend. 'He's lacking in basic arithmetic.' Ivan wiped spittle from Nancy's mouth with his handkerchief.

Marty lumbered over to the pool table. The only nurse on duty was in the back room behind reception and he could hear her on the phone so he knew he had a few safe minutes. He shoved his hands deep into his pockets and pulled out necklaces, earrings, pendants and brooches and set them down.

The glimmer of the jewels against the green felt of the pool table looked like tiny flowers dotting an alpine field. He spread them out and categorised them into groups by colour, size and worth. When he touched each piece, it was as if he offered a blessing.

'Three times three is 12. Four times six is 18. Nine times nine is 10.'

His hands worked with speed, making light tracks between the piles of ambers and sapphires, diamonds and emeralds. In the green pile were little earrings that he could hardly pick up with his lumpy fingers. In the orange section were two amber necklaces and a brooch, and in the red pile, four sets of ruby earrings. In the centre of his jewellery pie was a diamond solitaire in a white gold setting so breathtaking that he set it apart.

He marked down the categories in a notebook so he could work out the formulas later, but then two residents wandered up to the pool table.

'Woohoo, looky here,' one man said, tapping his cane on a leg of the pool table. 'Did you just return from the Klondike, mister?'

Marty turned his back on them.

'You opening up a jewellery shop?' the man with the cane asked, reaching for the crown jewel. Marty slapped his hand away, and spun to face them, keeping his back to the table and his arms extended out to the sides. Because of his height and slightly crossed eyes, the two men backed away.

'OK, buddy, no problem. You got some special girlfriend to be giving her all that loot?' 'Maybe it was his wife's?' The other wondered, as they drifted away. 'Oh yeah, or his mother's.'

Marty took a swatch of toilet paper from his pocket and tore off squares to wrap each jewel in. Between his nerves and thick fingers, he didn't notice a ruby earring fall to the floor. When he was done, he moved briskly away from the pool table and tapped the fish tank on the way back to his room.

At seven that evening, in her room, Millie was force-fed a plastic cup full of puréed prunes because the nurse had found the ones she had thrown away.

'There's nothing as close to heaven as being regular. You eat this up like a good girl and by tomorrow morning you'll feel like a million dollars,' Jemmy said. Millie winced as prune sauce squirted out of the side of her mouth. The nurse wiped her lips and showed Millie her lottery ticket for the 3 million jackpot.

'I could be back in the Philippines this time next week.'

'Take me with you?' Millie grabbed the nurse's hand.

'If you pray for me to win and I win, I'll take you.'

'It's a deal.'

The first image on the evening news was the painting of *Adele Bloch-Bauer I*, by Gustav Klimt, which Pierre had called *the golden woman*. When Pierre had taken Millie on holiday to Vienna, they strolled along arm in arm and he called her *my golden woman*.

The colours didn't show up on TV like the original she'd seen in Vienna's Belvedere Palace, but maybe that was her cataract. She remembered how overcome she was by Klimt's woman in her swirling gold robe, with jewels glimmering at her neck, bracelets on her arm and such sorrow in her eyes.

'The painting will be returned to its rightful owner, the Altmann family,' the newscaster stated. Millie nibbled on a chocolate cookie and turned up the volume.

'The niece of the Bloch-Bauer family will reclaim this and three other paintings that were illegally seized by the Nazis.'

Millie nodded when the niece came on to speak about the history of the paintings. She learned that the Holocaust Victim Compensation Fund in New York City worked to restore confiscated Jewish property to its rightful owners. Millie's own family had lost artwork belonging to her great-grandparents. Before the war, her parents had owned a dry-goods store in Warsaw, and when forced to evacuate, they left almost everything behind, including the family's silverware and two paintings of her great-grandmother. Millie's mother put her family at risk just to seize her own jewellery and the menorah. Did it mean that she, too, could reclaim her family's belongings?

Millie pulled open her dresser drawer to remove the cloth packages of jewels wrapped in handkerchiefs. The amber was dull in the evening light, the silver earrings with four emerald stones tarnished. A ruby was set in a gold heart and attached to a thin chain with a broken clasp.

That night she dreamt about towers of teeth. A soldier ordered her to look for gold fillings and put them into burlap bags to be melted down. Every time she got to the last tooth, the soldier came in with a wheelbarrow and dumped more on the concrete floor in front of her.

Then a new vision: a pile of jewels glimmered under an interrogation lamp. The lamp swung over the gems and each time she started to count them, an SS officer danced her in a tango. She left him and escaped into a tunnel, wearing a miner's lamp on her head. The sides of the earthen tunnel were inlaid with diamonds and she picked them out of the earth, cleaned them on her apron, and put them in her mouth.

Millie awoke, sucking at the air because she had been holding her breath. The blankets were on the floor and the window had blown open. Frigid air rushed in and chilled the soft powdered folds of her body. She lay awake for hours, tracking the shadows on the ceiling, and straining to recall the dream about jewels and work, about sorting and accounting. Her hands moved like sparrows over her breasts.

In the morning, she awoke to someone knocking at her door. It was Jemmy, who hadn't won the lottery.

'Millie, how are you this morning?'

'Good, very good. I feel more energetic today.'

Jemmy looked at the now eight plastic cups of prune purée.

'Give me French fries.'

Jemmy helped her out of bed. 'If you ate fries every day how would you keep your fine figure?'

'Listen,' Millie said. 'Let's make this work for both of us. You bring me a burger and fries and I'll eat that muck.' The nurse pulled Millie's nightgown off over her head and sponged her body with a steaming washcloth.

'Let's get you dressed. What's your colour today?'

Millie pulled a yellow skirt off a hanger and opened the drawer to take out some underwear. The jewels in the drawer fell to the side, and she looked up to see if Jemmy had seen, but the nurse was counting out her pills. Millie decided to take the jewels from the closet instead. She reached for a little box and handed it to the nurse.

'What's this?' Jemmy asked.

'Jewellery. To go with my outfit. And a little something for you.'

Jemmy opened the box to find five amber necklaces. 'Very pretty.'

'They were my mother's and this is only part of it,' Millie told her. 'There's more.' She pointed to the TV but the nurse's walkie-talkie went off.

'Oh, I have to get to Hazel's room for a little emergency. Here, let's pull up your stockings, zip up your skirt and slip this over your head. There, you're as good as gold.'

Jemmy left Millie with the open box of jewels in her hand.

'You forgot your necklace,' she called out, but Jemmy was already halfway down the hall. Millie closed the box and with trembling hands, slipped it between her sweaters on a shelf in the closet.

After lunch and before her nap, Millie went up to her room with the nurse.

'Just one more,' the nurse said, holding out the ninth daily pill Millie had to take for Parkinson's, nausea, dizziness and an upset stomach. One pill seemed to combat the next so that a war waged in her fragile stomach. Every time the nurse held out her palm with a new pill, Millie hunched her shoulders higher and ground her bony bum into the chair.

'They'll do your nails this afternoon,' the nurse offered. 'Coral, like a seashell.'

Millie held out her fingers, 'No more pink. It doesn't suit me.'

The nurse touched Millie's hair, as if it were the downy feathers on a baby bird. 'How about a new colour?' she asked, looking at the russet shade, turning copper at the temples.

'To look like Rita Hayworth? That would suit me fine.'

The nurse took her time brushing Millie's hair, and made Millie promise to go downstairs after for bingo. After the nurse left, Millie took her winter coat from her closet and laid it on her bed. The woollen coat was still in good shape and had kept its caramel colour. From the dresser, she took out ten handkerchief packages, each one stuffed with the jewellery Millie had saved. They looked like birthday presents, all tied up with yellow ribbons. With a nail file, she opened a small hole along an existing tear in the lining of the coat and squeezed the jewel packages through, each one dropping like an anchor to the bottom. This is what they had done in the war when fleeing over the Pyrenees on foot. No one would ever look in the lining of a coat and it made it easier to carry. She pushed more and more through, until she could see a bulge in the lining. When she tried to prise a second hole on the other side of the coat, her hands weren't strong enough to poke through the material and she dropped the nail file, unwittingly kicking it under the bed.

She hadn't thought to fill both sides evenly, though, and now the coat was lopsided and difficult to lift. Millie sat down and tears ran from her eyes. The only empty handkerchief in the room fluttered in her hands. Holding it to her nose, she inhaled its cotton scent, and gradually her breath became regular. She couldn't possibly take all the packages out again because her fingers wouldn't fit through the small hole. When she arrived in New York City, she'd have to cut open the lining to get to them out and then buy another coat. New York in the fall would require a warm coat.

Millie knew that if she didn't leave soon, she'd miss her train, so she filled a bag with clothes: two undershirts, a flowered skirt and white blouse for when she'd get that award for having survived the Holocaust and keeping her family's jewels safe; for being a heroine. There was a stain on the chest, but she could cover it with a brooch and no one would be the wiser. But the bag was too heavy and she worried that the nurses would see her carrying it out. She unpacked and stuffed underwear in her pockets and socks in her purse. She would wear the skirt, and layer all of her clothes like Heidi of the hills, and that way she would be warmer on the train.

There was a knock at her door and she ignored it, but when the knocking continued, she opened it to the blonde male nurse. He pushed his long hair away from his face. Millie stared into his light blue eyes, fringed with white eyelashes. 'Won't you come in, dear?' she said.

'How are you feeling, Millie?' His voice was all efficiency and politeness.

'What a smart boy to remember my name.'

He eyed the cups of prune purée on her bedside table.

'I can't keep up with you people,' she told him, shrugging.

The nurse smoothed out the covers on her bed, and held up the empty travel bag. 'Are you going somewhere?' he asked, fluffing her pillow.

Millie shook her head. 'If you would kindly help me get my coat on, I'm going to sit outside in the garden before bingo.'

'But it's starting now,' the nurse said. 'You'll miss it if we don't go down.' He hung her coat back in the closet and patted her shoulders, so she followed the young man as he steered her out of her room.

'Lock the door,' she said in an exaggerated whisper and heard the lock click into place. She imagined winning the jackpot in bingo, which she would save for the trip. Maybe then, she could sit in the dining car and have a hamburger.

After bingo, there was a tea break and they served chocolate chip cookies. Jemmy came over while Millie was pocketing a handful of them. 'Millie, you look lovely. How are you feeling, dear?'

Millie attempted a smile, which came out lopsided. The Filipino woman leaned over, 'How are you feeling today?' she yelled in her ear.

'I'm not deaf. I'm just fine, thank you very much,' Millie said, pushing away with her walker, her pockets bulging with cookies.

The fish were swimming Olympic laps in their tank and the little black one was winning. Beside the tank, in their cage the two parakeets were having a domestic squabble, the blue one losing feathers. 'It's not worth fighting about, whatever it is,' she told them. She'd learned that in life. 'You'll forget about it tomorrow.'

While watching the frenetic activity in the cage, her eyes drooped. Millie had tried to convince her son that the nurses drugged the tea and coffee to keep them quiet, but he just assumed old people were always tired. She lowered herself onto the floral sofa beside Marty.

'I need the packages,' she told him.

He nodded and put up seven fingers. 'They are categorised, organised, ready to go,' he said.

'Good work, Marty,' she said and relaxed. Within seconds, gravity pulled on her eyelids and her head lolled over onto the mathematician's shoulder. He looked down at her, expanded his chest and patted her head with his active fingers. He counted aloud the number of jewels he had categorized that day and was grateful to Millie for sharing them. She obviously trusted him. After a while, he had to go to the bathroom, so he got another resident to take over the shouldering, but Millie awoke.

'Where are we? Have we arrived?' She looked around, bleary-eyed at the floral walls. She'd dreamt about the spinning lights and sounds of Manhattan. The Jewish Organization would have booked her a hotel room by now and someone would be waiting for her at the train station. Had they received her letter already? She'd found one in the drawer of her bedside table, unstamped and unsent.

A full week passed before she remembered her plans. The weather had turned from dreary rain into crisp fall days – the leaves on the trees in the garden were yellow, orange and red. She joined the gardening club to dig up the annuals and plant tulip bulbs. The nurse who supervised them recommended they wear a coat and scarf.

When Millie rooted in the closet for her coat and couldn't find it, her breath became uneven and raggedy. She remembered the last time she had seen it was when she filled it like a piggy bank with jewels. Her bony fingers flittered and grasped each item until she found it, at the back with her summer clothes, hanging like a dead weight. She pulled it out and struggled to get her arms through the holes.

It was heavy indeed and worth more than its material. She felt for the bulge of jewelled packages, which had fallen to the bottom of the lining, hardly noticeable from the outside and the weight reassured her.

Millie looked at herself in the mirror, her hair a new shade of Rita

Hayworth auburn, and burnt sienna lipstick staining her bow lips: Sunset Boulevard-style. She arranged a gauzy scarf over her hairdo and felt as if she had wafted out of a women's magazine. In her purse, she had tucked the address written down from the TV, her acceptance speech for when they awarded her what she was owed, and the unmailed letter. If she posted it today, it would get there in time to make arrangements. They would be thrilled to see her. The office for Jewish restitution rights was on Fifth Avenue. The taxi driver would know how to find it.

She took a last look around her cramped room: at the replica posters of Klimt's *Adele Bloch-Bauer*, at the miniature violet plant on her dresser, at the 12 cups of prune purée on her bedside table, and at the telephone, which reminded her to call her son.

'Hello, Mother. How are you?'

'I'm still alive, if that's what you're asking.'

Phillip was a banker and did something with other people's money by putting it somewhere else to make them more money. It was a big change from the family business in Warsaw, when the customer paid for the items in his hand – flour, sugar, nuts and chocolate – with real money so the exchange was visible.

'Mother, I told you I can't speak at work.'

'How are little Sophie and Sean? Are they happy being back at school?'

'Everyone is fine. Listen, Mom—'

'Philip, will you bring me a hamburger?'

'Sure, sure. I'll call you later, OK?'

'I might not be here.'

'What do you mean?' Her son broke away to speak sharply to someone. 'Hold on a minute,' he told her.

He had never spoken to her like that. Millie thought about putting the phone down but he came back on the line.

'What did you just say?' he asked.

'I just wanted to, wanted to say good—I mean, hello.'

'Mother?'

'Oh, you know. If you tried to call I could be in the, in the toilet, or, or in the lounge.'

'What's going on?' Her son's voice had turned tight and impatient.
'Nothing. Everything is just fine. Say hello to the family. I haven't
seen them for so long.'

'We'll visit you soon,' he told her, but Millie had already hung up.
She was sweating with the heavy coat on. When she turned around,
she bumped into the side of the bed. The phone rang so she turned
the TV on with the volume up, and hurried out of the room.

There were no nurses in sight when she hobbled to the front door.
The only people in the lobby were half-dozing in front of the TV.
She thought about finding Yvette and Marty to say goodbye, but the
front doors of the residence automatically swung open and when a
rush of chilly air swept over her, she forgot. Millie stepped back into
the warm lobby, looked at the unmanned desk, and after a moment,
plunged forward again. It was drizzling out and she stood, in her
heavy winter coat with her overflowing purse, and looked up and
down the street. When a taxi came along, the driver noticed her light
hand waving from side to side.

'Where to, ma'am?'

'The station, please. The VIA rail train station.'

The driver helped her get into the back seat. 'Nice day to travel.
Better inside than out.'

'Yes, it's a good day for ducks.'

'Are you off to visit relatives?'

Millie held onto the door as he swerved around a corner. 'Yes,
that's right,' she said with delight. 'Relatives. My daughter. She lives
in Poland.'

'And you're taking a train to get there?' The driver burst out laughing. 'That's a good one.'

'I meant to say New York,' she told him.

He looked at her in the rearview mirror and abruptly stopped
laughing. Millie looked away and out the window.

'Oh, I didn't hear you properly. I'm sorry about that, ma'am.' He
looked up again, his eyes sober.

'And if you wouldn't mind,' she said. 'I would like you to look at
the schedule when we get there. My eyesight isn't very good anymore, and I'm sure you can tell me which train I should get on?'

'Absolutely. No problem at all, ma'am.' The driver nodded.

'I have a long trip ahead of me,' she said, pulling her coat closed around her. Millie sat back and looked out the window, watching as the city sped by her at an alarming rate.

9

Infertile Land

Rays of sunshine beamed on Lottie's back as she pulled up carrots in the garden. Lottie loved the heat; its warmth curled into her like wisps of smoke, filling the hollow space inside. That empty place where nothing rested for long.

She and Hank had been married for two years before discovering that, at the age of 23, she was barren.

It had taken her two years to get over it. When Lottie received a pamphlet in the mail from Save the Children, she smiled up at Hank, stroked his hand and slipped the glossy picture of a malnourished child under his eyes.

'We can afford to sponsor one. I've got savings from my parents,' she told him.

Her husband looked down at the image. 'Send 'em here so they can work for me on the farm,' he said. 'See how it is to feed themselves.'

Whenever she left one of these brochures out – pictures of naked children drying in the sun like fallen leaves – it would end up in the rubbish.

'I don't like seeing them pitiful eyes,' he'd say, shrugging. After he left the house, she'd rescue the child from the bin, smooth out its crinkled face and put it between books to flatten out.

So, this is it, she thought. Me, Hank and the carrots. She changed from her housecoat into old jeans and a work blouse, rolling up her sleeves and looking out at the expansive garden. This is it, the life Mother planned for me. Even after leaving this world, she got her way.

Her hands wove through the frilly greens, scraped into the peaty soil and dug around the top of each vegetable before giving it a good tug. *I should have married Gus.* Lottie pulled up carrot by carrot. *We'd be on the road now, exploring the country in his truck.*

She remembered a barn dance when she was 17 and Gus had grabbed her around the waist and lifted her up high in the air above the crowd, his cowboy hat whirling off like a Frisbee. Gus with a hand-rolled cigarette stuck to his fleshy bottom lip. Gus leaning against a wall, hat tipped forward, winking at her with eyelashes so long they brushed his cheeks. Gus nodding when he first saw her in a pink summer dress.

'Pink suits you like it suits a rose,' he'd told her in a low voice, tracing his finger along the scooped neckline while the heat rose in her face to match the word *pink*.

She spent the rest of her senior year unable to concentrate on the exams. She couldn't clear her mind of what he'd promised: 'You know it's my goal to see the world, and you – my Lot – are coming with me!'

When the summer arrived and it was time to follow him, her mother grounded her, for getting poor grades in her final geography and math exams. She added ironing and dusting to Lottie's list of chores and harassed her when she forgot to do them. Mother found so many reasons not to let her daughter go, especially with a man who would willingly abandon his family's land and take to the road. So Lottie had refused the one who would have been the love of her life.

After he left she floated around the house like a phantom for an entire year. Then her grief changed to fear when both parents developed cancer: Mother in the stomach, Father in the lungs, and she spent her nineteenth year taking care of them. If Lottie had ever had the courage to leave with Gus, she knew she would still have raced back home to nurse her ailing parents. It was the duty of an only child.

In the garden, she readjusted her bony knees between rows of Amsterdam Sweetheart. Yanking one out of the dirt, she dangled the stubby orange vegetable in the air. It was full of white holes, a sign of overwatering. The holes reminded her of eyes: big blank eyes watching her. Hank would drench the plants with the hose once a day so he didn't have to go out twice a day, which was what they recommended.

'Hank!' she called out towards the orchard beside the garden. She had to call again before he responded.

'What's up?' he yelled with one foot planted on the ladder, about to climb another tree.

'About the carrots—' she began.

'When's lunch on?' he hollered, cutting her off.

Oh darn, she thought, *Lunchtime already? We've only been out for three hours, with barely the morning gone by.* She squinted into the sun and waved a finger in the air at him. One finger, one hour. His broad-brimmed hat didn't cover a neck going pink from the summer sun. A cotton shirt burst open over his bulldog chest and his beer belly jellied over the waist of his jeans. *He must be sweating,* she thought, as the heat prickled her own back. *I'll sit him in the bath tonight.*

Then, out of the corner of her eye she saw something move – a flash of brown – but when she looked over there was nothing there. All morning she'd felt like she was being watched, but not by her husband. She dabbed her forehead with the end of the apron then continued digging and pulling at the stubborn vegetables, snapping off the green tops and throwing the carrots into a bucket. Hank was in charge of the orchards – apples, cherries and pears – while Lottie tended the vegetables – carrots, beans, cucumbers, tomatoes and lettuce. It was a good year for fruits, and an improved year for vegetables. They had covered the carrots in netting this time, after losing the last crop to the hungry root fly.

When Lottie looked back over, her husband was leaning against an apple tree, smoking a cigarette. She thought of how different the farm had been when his whole family worked it, long before she'd met him. It was Hank's inheritance from his father and grandfather. Their family had survived on pigs and produce, but now that his grandparents were gone, his mom had run off, and Dad was in a retirement home, it was all up to Hank. First thing he did was sell off the noisy, stinking animals and concentrate on fruits and vegetables instead.

'Now, I can do what I like with this place,' he explained to her one night at dinner. 'Meat goes through bad phases, but no one – I mean no one – gets tired of fruit and veggies,' he said, smothering butter over his carrots.

Now, after four years of marriage and adjusting to the news of their childlessness, they had been managing the farm for two years. But without family pressure, Lottie had learned that her husband could find any excuse to sit on the front porch and tilt back a beer, staring out at nothing.

'How many crates you pick so far?' she yelled out to him.

Without responding, he hoisted the ladder around to the other side of the tree, where she couldn't see him. But she had found ways to motivate him. The neighbours' gossip was one. She fanned the flames on that topic until he had no choice but to prove to those disbelievers, who were just waiting for him to run the farm into debt. Her morning fry-ups of eggs swimming in bacon fat gave him the energy to get out of bed each day, and her soothing pep talks and tireless hands kept them both going.

Lottie made a deal with herself that after she dug up 10 more edible carrots, she would move on to cucumbers and tomatoes. That morning, she'd only found 25 good ones and nearly twice as many rotten, but there were rows and rows of green tops ahead of her, just waiting for attention. Scooping up the damp soil, she let the earth fall through her thin fingers.

Moments later there was another movement at the edge of the garden and a brown, furry creature popped his head out of a burrow and scampered to the surface. Sitting back on his haunches, he cleaned his whiskers with tiny paws that resembled leather gloves. The groundhog stared at her with beady, black eyes and she stared right back. He seemed mesmerised by her red-and-yellow-striped blouse. His nose twitched and his whiskers danced, then he scampered back into his hole.

Once, they had seen nearly a dozen of them sitting on the gravel driveway, chattering away. It had looked like a groundhog reunion.

'They're overgrown rats,' Hank had told her.

'I think they're cute,' she'd said.

'Watch this.' He had stamped the ground with his heavy boots. 'See how scared they are?'

She had never seen these animals before she moved to the farm two years earlier and now there was an entire village of them living below the soil. Lottie would scrunch down to peer into their dirt holes. While they lived in tightly packed dens under the ground, she and Hank rattled around in their four-bedroom farmhouse.

Lottie served up a heaping plate of lunch and they sat down at the red-and-white Formica table. 'That's mighty good grub, honey.' Bits of carrots spewed from Hank's mouth while he spoke. 'I remember when you used to cook from cans but you're gourmet now.'

'I'm trying out that new cookbook,' she told him. 'It's giving me ideas on how to use herbs and things.' Lottie pushed her peas and carrots into a line on her plate. Hank eyed her untouched food. 'If you ain't eating your veggies, pass them over. I've got room.'

The book recommended lunch to be the hearty meal of the day so she always made enough for four, as if she were feeding the kids they couldn't have. And Hank ate it all: two hamburgers with spicy marinade, brown beans with pork, steamed carrots, stewed tomatoes, canned peas, cornbread with molasses and berry pie and ice cream for dessert.

Hank used a slice of cornbread to mop his plate clean. He sucked back on a bottle of beer while she sipped a glass of cool water. The lacy curtains caught gusts of wind and batted at the window frame. The grandfather clock killed time. Lottie had barely touched her meal by the time he was finished.

'You've got to get more in you. Before you disappear,' he said, reaching over to tilt her chin up so she'd meet his eyes. 'Doctor said it's important you fill up.'

'Oh, I've never been one for food, you know that.' She shrugged. 'But ice cream. I could eat ice cream all day.' She reached for her empty dessert bowl as if to prove it.

'You'll rot your teeth, sweetheart,' he said, grabbing the table with his man-hands. Hands he used to climb up rusty ladders, twist apples off sharp branches, mix chemical fertilisers and turn soil over in the garden. 'I'm going to lie down,' he told her and, pushing his chair back, shifted his body weight to rise. When he stood he towered over her at 6'1". 'You tired?' She shook her head. He smiled, showing off glistening, pink gums. 'You're a gem, you know that?'

'You're not so bad yourself,' she replied, and looked away because she couldn't help but replace his face with that of another. Hank went up the creaky, wooden stairs to the bedroom while Lottie scraped her leftover lunch into a Tupperware, knowing that he would finish it off later.

Some nights she would cook dinner later to force him to work longer and then reward him with a game of cards in the evening. The most they'd bet was five dollars, but whenever she won he called her 'my little queen' over and over, teasing her until she pinched his arm to make him stop.

Most nights he'd sit beside her on the sofa, holding her hand until the end of the 10 o'clock news. Then they'd get into his parents' old bed, the one he was born in 27 years before, with its squeaky springs and tarnished copper bedposts. Hank would take her body in his calloused hands and bore into her small frame.

So this is it, she thought. *This is it, it, it.*

If she let it, the rhythm of his movement relaxed her and she pictured the garden in her head, full of feathery carrot tops shimmering like floating sea-life. And the secret chattering of the groundhogs was there, right under the house.

After Lottie's miscarriage she began to dream even more about Gus. It had been seven years since his eyes had burned a goodbye tattoo into hers. Since he'd tipped his suede cowboy hat, honked the horn and pulled out onto the highway. Then Lottie had walked away from the empty road and into her mother's open arms. 'Shh,' her mother had whispered in her ear. 'You'll find a local boy, dear.'

And her prophecy came true. While Gus was out west delivering canola to Alberta and BC, Lottie lost both her parents to cancer, one after the other, and at the age of 20 became an orphan.

'We're so sorry for your loss,' a local farmer's wife told her during her mother's funeral. The woman patted Lottie on the back, and then pushed her overweight nephew towards her, leaving them alone in the funeral parlour. Hank had been only two years ahead of Lottie in school, so she recognised him. She remembered hearing how his mother had run away, leaving an elderly father to take care of two sons. How Hank's elder brother went to the city to try to find their mother and never came back.

'I'm sorry about your parents,' he'd whispered, looking down at the floor.

'Thank you,' she'd said, gripping onto her mother's casket. 'I don't know what...'

'To do?' he asked, glancing at her face all shiny with tears.

Lottie held a tissue up to her nose while Hank stood as still as possible beside her. He looked down at the waxen figure in the casket and saw the bright-pink cheeks and lips, as if she were blushing with shame at her own death. This woman, who had never worn make-up when she was alive.

'They seemed like, like real nice folks,' he said.

'I didn't think Dad would go first,' she said, looking at Hank through blurry eyes, 'but when Mom got worse it was too...' She bowed her head, rested her forehead on her mother's stomach and stayed like that for a long time.

'You know,' he took a deep breath. 'I don't really have my folks either,' he said. 'I guess that puts us in the same boat.'

Lottie held a tissue to her nose and looked up at Hank. He moved a step closer. Six months later, at 21, she married him in the town chapel and the same people who'd been at the funeral attended the wedding. They lived with Hank's aunt for two years and then moved into the farmhouse and began the hard work of keeping the farm alive.

Half a year after the wedding, she got a postcard all the way from Vancouver, British Columbia, which she hid behind the spice rack in the kitchen. It was a picture of mountains and the ocean and looked like a setting for a movie. On the back, he'd written in a small, scrawling hand: *Dear Lot, I have found my place in this world and it's on the road. I've seen Canada from coast to coast! It's lonely sometimes but you're always on my mind and the CB radio helps too. Yours, Gus.*

She often imagined herself sitting in the cab with him, up high above the other cars and barrelling down the freeway. The road, a wide band of shining silver stretched out in front of them. Gus's warm, heavy hand would rest on her thigh. Instead, every Saturday, she and Hank drove in his spitting Chevy to the market to sell their produce. Hank liked to turn on the CB radio rather than music, and Lottie would listen to the voice snippets cross each other in the crackling air.

'Farmer Joe, here,' Hank announced his nickname. 'Is that you, Bill?' he said, connecting to an anonymous pal. Sometimes they'd only speak a few words, and at times it was in a code language that she didn't understand.

'I thought that radio was used only by the locals?' she asked him after they heard someone speaking a foreign language she thought was Russian.

'That's right. It usually covers the local area but it's been known to pick up talk from across the country.' He explained to her, his eyes alight.

'So, would truckers use it, then? To talk to each other?' she asked, conscious that her hands were trembling. Hank didn't know the story of Gus.

'You're a smart cookie,' he replied. 'That's the best use for it, in my opinion, but it's good for emergencies too. I just like to play around on it.'

Lottie's dreams became more vivid and whenever she heard a deep voice on the CB it made her shiver with pleasure. 'Where do you think that one's from?' she'd ask. But there was no way of knowing. She convinced Hank to take her on regular Sunday afternoon drives and besides the foreign sounds of cracking and popping they'd keep quiet in the car. She was sure if she listened hard enough, she could will Gus to speak to her.

'Lottie… *blip bleep*… Lot McPhee… *buzz*,' she thought she heard once. 'You are the prettiest… *bleep bleep*.' She looked over at Hank to see if he had heard, but he was staring ahead at the road.

On each ride, Lottie collected sounds as if they were precious jewels she could hold in her hand. Piecing together mumbles and sighs, she assembled them into a puzzle. Once, when Hank wanted to listen to music and couldn't tune into a radio station, he banged the dashboard with his hairy fist. 'I'm getting tired of listening to other people's business,' he told her. But since he couldn't tune in to music, he left the thing on. All at once there was an explosion of bleeps and Hank sped up, while Lottie looked out the window. She heard a male voice, loud and clear, 'I'm gonna... git ya.' She looked out at the passing fields and heard: '...in my arms...' She looked at the broken-down farmhouse. 'Where you belong... buzz.' Then she saw a group of horses cantering. 'I'll throw ya in my truck and we'll...' She twisted her fingers in her lap. '...we'll drive the world over.' That was him alright, she was sure of it. She felt her stomach burning and the heat spreading up her neck.

'Did you hear that?' she asked Hank in a casual voice, while her heart splintered in her chest.

'What's that?' he replied, slowing down to open a pack of chewing gum.

'A voice. Someone saying... something. I don't know,' she told him.

'Wasn't paying attention,' he said, flicking the CB off. 'Might get rid of that damn thing. Too much noise, not enough talk.' Lottie opened her mouth to say something, but stopped.

That night, when they got home from visiting Hank's aunt and uncle in the next town, he skidded the Chevy into the gravel driveway and dashed into the house; after half a case of beer he was desperate for a bathroom. Lottie stayed in the car, fingering the silver keys that dangled in the ignition. She thought about how easy it would be to start, even though she'd never learned to drive. Her father believed that women weren't made for driving, but that wouldn't have stopped her. She could hitchhike or take a bus; there was no excuse why not. She wondered how long it would take her to find the truck – with the outline of a naked woman on its mudflaps – and the man with the brown cowboy hat at its wheel.

Lottie turned the key in the ignition, picked up the CB and blew into it, scattering dust. Keying the mic, just as she'd seen Hank do it, she imagined Gus's broad hand shuffling the hair out of his eyes, his grin cracking open. *Maybe*, she thought, *he'll have his radio turned on too.* She made up her own nickname, remembering that Hank had called it a 'handle', and it was needed to communicate with others. She spoke her nickname, *Groundhog*, into the CB and the lights on the radio flashed. At first she spoke only in a whisper. 'Gus, are you out there?' A thin strain of sound came out of the speaker.

'Can you hear me?' There was a low hum.

'It's been seven years and I was only a girl. Eighteen when you left.' Her knuckles turned white from gripping the device. Outside, twilight arrived and turned the sky from a light blue to a faded grey. Looking out the dashboard window, she saw little groundhog heads popping out of their dens. Then a current of voice came out of the radio: 'Burr... lil' missy... burr... buzz,' and a hundred other mixed-up sounds. Lottie smiled at the crossing strains of buzz and whoosh and fuzz.

'It's me, your little Lot calling,' she said loud and clear. 'The love of your life.'

She hunkered down into the Chevy, making the upholstery squeak, and talked on and on until she felt the hollow space inside her filling up with warmth. When the windows steamed up she drew circular patterns on the foggy glass.

'I've wanted to tell you... to say...' She put a fine hand to her cheek and stroked it the way he used to. 'I was only a girl and I didn't understand.' She nodded. 'But now I do.'

Hank had not come out to get her, and the lights were still off. All she could see was a dark, shadowy outline of where they lived. There were still pots to scrub and the ironing and laundry to put away. She gripped the CB and swallowed the soft plum that had caught in her throat.

'My parents were...' Her voice quickened. 'They needed me.' Her face was bathed in tears. 'I wish I... could go back in time... I wanted to.' She licked at the salty drops around her mouth. 'I wanted to... to be... on the open road. With you,' she said in a choked voice.

When she rolled down the window to get some air, she watched the designs she'd drawn in steam disappear. The sky had turned from a light grey wash to a deep purple stain. The outline of the barn in front of her and the grove of apple and pear trees beside it were just barely visible. She heard the groundhogs' chatter, but couldn't even see them now.

After Lottie told Gus everything she could imagine telling, she took a deep breath and heard the static-free hum on the radio. The night air wafted in the window, cooling her face. Then she smoothed out her skirt, looked at herself in the rearview mirror and was surprised to see her eyes so shiny. She released herself from the car and stepped gingerly onto the gravel drive.

Closing the car door, she thought of the next afternoon when Hank would go to town for a Farmer's Union meeting. She could check the bus schedule. She thought of what she would pack and how long it would take her to get ready. But first she'd make Hank a pot of beef and carrot stew to last the week. Until he could make other arrangements.

Lottie crept up the drive towards the dark house, and the groundhogs scurried behind her. When she turned around to catch them out, they stopped and looked away, all except for one little guy. This one raised his dark eyes to hers and under the light of the moon she saw his tiny mouth moving. This one wasn't afraid to communicate with her in his language. Telling her to go.

PART III

London

10

Call Me Bernie

The girl with the brown hair – or sienna, as her mother called it – curling around her shoulders, leaned in closer. Cars and double-decker buses crawled beside them in the morning rush hour, making a racket.

'I'm sorry? What did you say?' The girl blew a bright-pink bubble the size of her face and then popped it with a manicured nail. She peeled the gum off her nose and plopped it back into her mouth. The elderly woman watched it all and then, with shaky hands, smoothed down wisps of silvery hair.

'I didn't hear what you said,' the girl yelled. She would be late for work; it was already five minutes later than she should have left.

The woman put both hands out, open-palmed, as if waiting for an offering. Her fingertips were stained yellow.

'Mrs Maddens,' the woman said, looking directly into the girl's eyes. 'I lost her,' she said and rolled the sleeves of her blue tracksuit into donuts around her elbows.

The girl tried to remember the last time a stranger had spoken to her. Asked her for something. Most just stared. Most were men looking at her skinny body, at her poking-out ribs, as if she were a collection of prime ribs at an all-you-can-eat barbecue. 'What's the address? Tell me the address, quick.'

The girl would have to make up an excuse. The modelling agency hadn't called her, not even once, so she had to take this temp job at an ad agency. Temporarily. Her parents had sent her another allowance even after she had told them she was 21 now and could take care of herself. A double-decker bus barrelled by, spouting a cloud of exhaust into their faces. They both coughed.

'I had it here,' the woman said and opened and closed her hands, then did it again. She fumbled in her pockets. 'Maddens. Mrs Maddens, you know?' Her voice had a soft lilt to it and the girl guessed she might be Irish.

'Look, I'm sorry,' the girl flipped her long bangs out of her eyes, 'but I gotta get to work.'

The woman looked skyward and smiled, and then, as if hearing instructions from the divine, pulled out the linings of her pockets. Lint and used matches fell to the pavement.

'Is Mrs Maddens a friend or family member?' The girl thought of her own family and how they'd tried to convince her not to go to London, predicting she'd be back in her mirror-filled bedroom in Toronto by the end of the year. No way. If they were going to challenge her, then no way: she'd show them.

'Are you sure it's on Oxford Street?' the girl asked, raising her eyebrows, which made her look like a department-store mannequin, all alabaster-smooth. Whenever she wore too much make-up for a photo shoot she thought of a clown at a kid's birthday party, although her oversized features were coveted and, with make-up, became even larger, as if seen under a magnifying glass or underwater. That's how she felt this morning: blurry and unclear. She just had to get to work. This time when she blew a bubble she smashed it flat against her mouth so that it made a loud pop. 'I don't think anyone actually *lives* on this street. It's Oxford Street,' she explained. 'Except maybe in the hostel, but besides that it's just McDonald's, Pret A Manger, clothing stores, stuff like that.' The girl looked at her reflection in the gift shop window in front of her. Turned sideways she was as thin as a scarecrow but what she saw was model material and that's what the agency told her too. Why weren't they calling, then? The elderly woman beside her was also thin, but baggy and bedraggled and ancient.

'Sorry,' the girl said and turned away. But the woman grabbed on to her jacket and the girl was shocked at her strength. They made eye contact again and there was something familiar about the elderly woman's eyes. They had the summer lake in them, like dark, glossy water, and she smelled like lavender and cigarettes, like the girl's favourite aunt, Lisa, who had passed away.

'Hey, tell you what: why don't we go inside the hostel and I'll ask at the front desk, OK?' the girl said and, having made a decision, blew the wad of gum onto the street, the pink blob nearly hitting a one-legged pigeon. 'Sorry, birdie,' she said.

When they reached the red doors with the brass plate reading YWCA, the woman stopped. 'Is this where you live?'

'Yep,' the girl said, flashing a smile.

'You said that no one lived on this street.'

'Except at the hostel, but I'm only here temporarily. Until I make it big, you know, and then I'll move to – what's it called? – that neigh-bourhood where they made the movie with Julia Roberts.' The girl bounded up the stairs, two at a time. The woman held onto the iron railing and followed. When they reached the front desk, the woman took the girl's hand and fused it to her own.

'Oh,' the girl said, looking down at their hands. And by then, it was too late to escape. She was bound to help.

As the girl looked up she saw the receptionist disappear around the corner. The girl would never do that to a customer at her temp job. She was always ready with a smile and lots of eye contact at the ad agency. The guys loved that.

'It is your job to welcome our clients, make them feel welcome. You're the first point of contact, the first person they see, so: eye contact and smiles all around.' Her boss had drilled that into her from day one. 'Do whatever it takes for them to want to come back and give us their patronage.' He'd winked at her, and when she burst out laughing he fiddled around with a tissue as if he had something in his eye.

'Do you think they'll consider me as a model for one of the ads?' she'd asked her boss.

'If you stick around and prove yourself useful, it could happen,' he said.

That was motivation enough.

Now, with her free hand, the girl tapped her blue manicured fin-gernails on the front desk. Her left hand, which was snapped shut in the woman's hand, was heating up. When the girl tried to pull it back, the woman tightened her grip and locked her thumb over the girl's thumb.

'OK,' the girl said, and cried out towards the back room: 'Hello?'

'Hello,' the woman beside her echoed.

'We need help out here.'

'Help,' the woman whispered, smiling at the girl, complicit.

The hostel foyer smelled of bleach and lemon. The girl pushed on the brass bell, *ting-ting*, and the woman's eyes lit up. The girl ran her finger over the dusty floral arrangement on the desk. The woman stared at the bell. The girl rang again, *ting-ting*, and then the old woman reached for the tiny bell and pushed on it more times than they could count: *ting-ting-ting-ting-ting*. Still, no one came to help them. The woman smiled at the girl as if they were at a tea party. As if this was fun. By now, the girl's new boss would be slicking back his eyebrows, hitching up his pleated trousers and making his way to the front desk. To train her, as he'd called it on her first day. It was the longest training she'd ever had for a job. He stank of stale coffee and once he even had jelly from his morning donut on his lips. His hair glistened with gel. His hand had brushed her breast. 'Oopsy, sorry about that. I was just trying to… Pass me those files, would you, love?'

She was going to stay in the job this time, either until the ad guys gave her work or the modelling agency she had signed with gave her a first chance. Once the photographers got to know her, the ad guys, maybe even the film and commercial people, then she'd be in the door. One leg in the door. One of her six-foot-two legs in someone's door. That much she knew for sure.

The clock above the front desk showed 8.45am, which meant she had only 15 minutes before she was supposed to be sitting at the McBrodie and Co front desk, welcoming the incoming executives, opening the mail with the mail knife and answering the phone in a sparkling voice. Now she would have to spend her lunch money on a cab. The girl tried to wrench her hand out of the woman's grip.

'Can you… just let go?'

The woman was staring at the carpet. 'Flowers,' she said. Swirls of red and yellow patterns came together before exploding like fireworks, until the remnants met up again somewhere else to create another flower.

'Cool carpet,' the girl said, and then yelled to the back room, 'I can hear you back there!' But no one came out. 'Bitch,' the girl said and pulled the woman back outside. It was 8.47am now.

They saw a policeman on the street. 'Hey, let's ask him,' the girl said and dragged the woman upstream through the crowds, jostling people on the way, but as they approached, he took off after a teenage boy who'd broken into a run. Shoplifting, no doubt. There was lots of that in London, but how often did you see the street chase?

'Check it out!' the girl said to the woman, who looked up at her as if this were normal. When they stepped into a store entrance to take a break from the swarms of pedestrians, the woman handed her a scrap of paper with 80 Oxford Street written on it.

'Hey, right on: you found your address,' the girl said. Now she could complete her good deed of the day, but it'd have to be quick so she wouldn't be too late.

They walked a few more blocks and the girl thought it was a good thing she didn't know anyone in this city or she would be totally embarrassed seen holding hands with an old woman. They passed Pret A Manger and Mango – there was a new purple dress in the window – then Burger King, McDonald's, and WH Smith. When they reached number 80, they discovered a narrow shop called *You Jewel*. Inside, the sales clerk was doing a sudoku puzzle.

'Hi. We're looking for a Mrs Maddens,' the girl said.

The clerk shook her head, 'Not heard of her.'

'What's the address here?'

Without lifting her eyes, the clerk tapped the pile of business cards on the counter. The girl held the card up to the elderly woman whose gaze had drifted off to the display cabinets. They were at 80 Oxford Street.

Each case was full of costume jewellery with ruby-red earrings and bracelets dangling from plastic hooks, and Swarovski animals arranged beside nose rings.

'That,' the woman said, pointing to a faux diamond bracelet. 'I want that.'

The clerk looked up, and then down again at her puzzle.

The girl whispered, 'I don't even know your name.'

But the woman was far away in her mind, fixated on a case full of sparkly toe rings.

'Mine's Tina.' The girl said louder. 'What's yours?'

'Bernadette. Bernadette Highcroft,' the woman said, nodding. 'But call me Bernie.'

'OK, Bernie, listen up, I think Mrs Maddens gave you the wrong address or moved or something. And I really, *really* have to go.' Tina tried to shake her hand free but the woman squeezed harder.

'Please don't,' Bernie said.

'But you're hurting me.' Bernie released her grip slightly, but without letting go. Outside, they had to back against the store façade as another onslaught of pedestrians sped past.

'It's only my second week. He'll fire me if I'm late.' She noticed she'd started speaking to the woman as if she were babysitting her, the way her mom spoke to her geriatric patients at the hospital.

Bernie pulled out the scrap paper again. 'Eighty Oxford Street. Mrs Maddens. Eighty, eighty.'

'Stop it. Let go. You're crushing my bones,' Tina said.

Bernie shook her head. 'No. No.' Sweat beads were pearled on her upper lip. She really did look like Tina's aunt.

'OK, you know what?' Tina said. 'I'm taking you home. Where do you live?'

The woman pulled a simple string out from under the neck of her sweatshirt and let the key at the end of it dangle all the way down her stomach. 'Ring Shirley. She'll know what to do.'

Tina looked down at the key and noticed that Bernie wasn't wearing a bra and her breasts drooped down to her belly. Would her own breasts be like that one day? No way would she let that happen.

Tina lifted the key, careful not to touch any part of Bernie's body. She turned it over to look for an address or phone number but it was bare; the key company name was worn down to illegible. Tina pulled Bernie over to a red phone booth and Bernie squeezed in behind her but then the door couldn't fully close.

'Dial 0208-655-3306,' Bernadette said, while pushing buttons. The girl took out a pound and dropped it in the slot. She pushed Bernie's fingers away and dialled, but after five rings she put the phone down and collected her coin.

'Try again. 0208-655-6603,' Bernie said.

'But that's a different number.' Tina dropped her chin to her chest. 'Oh.

My. God. I can't do this,' she said and pushed Bernie out of the phone booth. Bernie shuffled out backwards but wouldn't let go of the girl's hand. No matter how hard Tina tried, she couldn't be free of the woman's grip.

'I won't go anywhere. I promise,' Tina begged but Bernie wouldn't release her so Tina used her free hand to dial the new number. This time the phone rang two times before someone picked up.

'Hello?' A woman with a sharp voice answered. Tina couldn't hear over the street noise and she managed to close the phone booth door up to their bonded hands.

'Hello? Is anyone there?' the voice asked.

'Yeah, oh yeah. Hi.'

'Who's on the line?'

'My name's Tina and—'

'Who?'

'You don't know me, but I have your friend here or maybe she's family? Your mom or your aunt or someone?'

'Who is that?'

Bernie was staring at her from the crack in the phone box door, breathing heavily.

'Is this a prank call?' the woman said.

'No. No. Please. I'm from Canada and…' She held the receiver under her chin and with her free hand scratched her knee. 'Well, here I am on Oxford Street with Bernie.'

'Who?'

'Bernadette?'

'Highcroft.' Bernadette spoke through the crack in the phone booth door.

'Bernadette Highcroft,' Tina said, her voice edgy and impatient. She was going to be so late and so in trouble.

There was a gasp on the other line, then silence. Bernie pulled on Tina's hand and Tina pulled back.

'Who are you really?' The woman's voice was clipped; Tina imagined a small mouth.

'My name is Tina and I'm from Canada. I work as a temp at McBrodie and Co but really I'm a model. This morning a woman named Bernadette Highcroft asked me for help: she's looking for a Mrs Maddens, but honestly,' Tina lowered her voice. 'She seems a little bit – you know, lost. Are you Mrs Maddens?'

There was another silence, then a crack in the woman's steady breathing and a sniffle.

'Ma'am? Are you still there?' Tina said.

'I don't know who you are or why you keep disturbing me but I do not need to be reminded of my loss.'

Tina wiped sweaty wisps of hair from her forehead. The phone box was becoming a hot box. 'What do you mean?'

'Do I make myself clear?' the woman said in a way that reminded Tina of the biology teacher she'd hated.

'Hey, don't shoot the messenger,' Tina said; she had heard that expression on TV, some murder mystery show. 'Look, I'm only trying to help and it's costing me my job.'

'I do not find this amusing in the least, and if you keep harassing me, I'll report you to the police, I've had just about enough.'

A Starbucks worker came out of the coffee shop by the phone booth to pass out scone samples and Bernie reached across the side-walk for one, pulling Tina to the glass door on which she smacked her head.

'Jesus! Stop it, Bernie!'

'I'm going to put the phone down now,' the woman warned.

Bernie yanked at Tina's hand. 'Stop it,' Tina said, yanking her back. 'Sorry, not you,' she said into the phone. 'All I am trying to do is help the woman. Maybe she had a stroke or something since she doesn't know where she is or where she's going… and neither do I.'

'I'll tell you where she is,' the woman said in her tight voice. 'Six feet under the ground.'

There was a hard click on the line followed by a harsh dial tone. When Tina slammed the receiver down, it bounced back and hit her in the chest. She left the receiver dangling and dug her nails into Bernie's palm until Bernie yelped and was forced to let go. Then Tina slammed the phone booth door shut, closing herself in. Bernie hurled herself against the door, cheek against glass. Scone crumbs from the Starbucks sample peppered her mouth. Tina had trouble breathing in the hot box; she still heard the tight, aggressive voice in her ears. She watched a shudder move through Bernie's body before her eyes rolled back and she fell down, her grey head hitting the curb. Tina tried to get out of the booth to help but Bernie's splayed body blocked the door. People rushed in and surrounded the fallen woman until Tina couldn't even see Bernie for the crowd around her. The energy drained out of Tina's feet and her legs became rubber and could no longer hold her up. Her ears rang and filled with a long hollow sound, and then she, too, fell.

When she came to, someone had moved Bernie's legs away from the door and a stranger had entered the phone booth and was cradling Tina's head and gently slapping her cheek. A policeman directed traffic past the scene. When the ambulance arrived, they carted the woman onto a stretcher and Tina motioned to go with her.

'Does your mother need any medication?' the rescue worker asked but Tina had no voice in her and merely shook her head, her dry lips quivering.

'She hasn't got any ID on her,' he said.

'Well, she's my aunt,' Tina said, and then sat on a stretcher beside Bernie's stretcher in the back of the ambulance. She reached over and held Bernie's hand. She'd never been in an ambulance and with each sharp turn her body was thrown from side to side but she made sure not to let go of Bernie, who looked as if she were just sleeping even with the plastic tube running up to a needle in her arm, her mouth covered by an oxygen mask.

Tina thought how none of this would have happened if she had stepped out of the hostel that morning a minute earlier, or later as was her bad habit. How none of this would have happened at all. Sitting up straighter, she breathed in deeply and got another hint of lavender and cigarettes and didn't feel so fuzzy anymore. Or so lonely. She leaned over Bernie and the woman opened her eyes and smiled. Gently, Tina untied the string around Bernie's neck and tucked the key into her own pocket. Then she lay back, closed her eyes, and let herself be driven down Oxford Street.

11

Un-United / Re-United

SHEIKH DR ABRAN. African Spiritual Healer. Gifted from Almighty God

Let Sheikh Abran change your worries to a peaceful mind. He has over 20 years' experience helping with relationship problems, family fights, inheritance injustice, marriage wishes, divorce cases, health woes, exam success, good business, bad luck, evil eyes and bad spirits. He is at your service with flexible prices. Call for appointment 020 7247 99433 Whitechapel, London E1

Catherine held the business card up to the African woman in the midnight-blue hijab who opened the door. The woman stared at Catherine as if she'd had a shock and, after a moment, stepped aside to let Catherine in, leading her down an unlit hall in the apartment. At first Catherine hesitated, but then followed, passing a kitchen, where she held her breath to ward off the mingled scents of what smelled like stewing leather and burning sugar. The woman stopped further along the hall at an open door to a room that had clothes thrown on the bed, a poster of the rapper Mos Def and pairs of Nikes lined up along the wall.

'My son,' the woman said, giving a quick smile before she pulled the door closed. Catherine followed her down the dark hall to the furthest room, which had a line of light seeping out from under the closed door. The woman rapped on it and Catherine observed the small ray of light that fell on their feet: the woman's rubber flip-flops and Catherine's loafers. The woman's breath came heavily, as if she'd just gone up some stairs while Catherine's breath was shallow, as she wondered what she was doing in this dark hallway in a stranger's house.

There was a mumbling from behind the door and the woman adjusted her headscarf and then opened the door to reveal a room saturated with light. Catherine had to squint to make out the outline of the seated figure against a window. The woman steered Catherine into the room and left her there, closing the door with a firm click. When Catherine's eyes readjusted, the outline took the shape of an imposing African man in a pillbox-shaped hat. He was motioning for her to enter with his lean arms outstretched on his wooden desk, palms facing up, and swathed in bright-white material that puffed around him as if he were half-submerged in a lake.

Catherine held up the calling card given to her outside the Whitechapel tube station. 'You're Sheikh Dr Abran?'

The man nodded. 'Sit down, dear one,' he said, in a baritone voice so warm it caused her to smile when she had nothing to smile about.

'Someone gave me this.' She put the card on his desk and perched on an office chair that was far too large for her.

Sheikh Dr Abran pulled out a notepad. 'Name?'

'Catherine Tower.'

He wrote it down and looked up at her. 'Thank you for coming to see me.' His gaze was unwavering.

'Yes, I called earlier, I wasn't sure if I should, but I…' She stopped speaking and crossed her legs. Why had she come? Was she so clearly out of possibilities?

'Catherine?' he said in a calm voice.

She didn't answer right away until he repeated her name. 'Yes?' she said.

He leaned over the desk, getting close to her face; she glanced away and then back. His eyes were dark brown with a blue edge around the irises. She looked down at the floor.

'Your eyes are clear, Catherine, but your head is in darkness. Chin, strong. Jaw locked. You do this while sleeping?' He made the movement of grinding his teeth. She nodded. 'Your jaw is a big stone,' he told her.

'Well, now that you mention it, I do have a tight jaw. I'm a grinder when I sleep.'

'Worries make illness. Turn sideways.'

Catherine wheeled around on the office chair to show him her profile. She should have gone back to her therapist, Dr Taylor, and given him another chance, or continued at the clinic that did acupuncture, or even bought that latest book from the renowned Dr Wick on grieving. But no, she'd taken a chance, come here instead, wanting to shake up her usual pathways.

Sheikh Dr Abran was asking her a question. 'You have love problems; you lose love, you become un-united?'

'No, no. That's not why I came here.'

The sheikh scratched under his hat with an unusually long pinkie nail. 'We are all – how to say – altogether connected. Like stars in the sky make the Big Dipper.'

'Sorry?'

'Everything in our self is connected. Cannot separate problem one from two.'

'Oh.' Catherine picked up the business card and fiddled with the corners of it. 'OK, but I'd like to speak to you about something else.'

He slid his finger around the rim of his water glass. 'Listen.' It created a hollow, tremulous ring. 'Everywhere is music. Everything in connection.' He seemed content with that. 'Tell what trouble is, dear one. If not love problems then promotion at working department, or troubling court case? Many court cases in London.'

Catherine looked away and took a deep breath. He turned over a list and read from it: 'You suffering from man-woman problems?'

Catherine shook her head. He made an X on a little box on the paper and tried again: 'Home business not successful?'

'No, not that. I have a permanent job at the library.' She pulled a mint from her purse while he made another X. When he looked up his eyes widened.

'Oh, no, no, no,' he said, shaking his head. 'No white poison. That's part of the problem.'

'It's just a sweet,' Catherine said. 'Would you like one?'

'A poison-body-sweet.'

She dropped the candy back into her bag and checked her watch. Seven minutes had passed since she'd first knocked on the door. What was she thinking?

'You uncomfortable, you eat. Common solution, but unsuccessful. Tell me, Catherine, what is it you want healing? This is my job. How can I help you?'

Catherine looked around the room; she watched dust motes whirl in the rays of sunshine over his shoulder. 'It's... it's my family.' She dabbed at her eyes to stop the tears from forming. They sat in silence for a moment.

'Your family un-united,' he said in a low, gentle voice. 'You want to re-unite?'

'Yes, I suppose that is the right word, to *re-unite*.'

'Sheikh Abran understands.'

'It's my aunt, actually.' Catherine's chest tightened, as if she couldn't get enough oxygen and she stood up, but his serene face angling up at her made her sit down.

'Take deep breaths. Go slow.'

She took a water bottle from her purse. 'It's really – I'm sorry. It's hard to talk about.'

He held up his two index fingers in the air. 'Connect?' he said, putting them side by side together. 'Disconnect?' He separated them from each other.

'Yes.' Catherine took a gulp of water. 'My aunt and I haven't spoken in... Two years? She refuses.' She took another drink of water and it spilled down the front of her blouse.

'Here,' he said, offering a cotton handkerchief from a wooden box on his table. She noticed there were many handkerchiefs neatly ironed and stacked.

'Thank you.' She took it and dabbed at her blouse.

'What is the trouble with Auntie?'

She held the cotton up to her nose and smelled cedar and citrusy laundry detergent. 'Are you really a sheikh?' she asked. There were no certificates, proof of his education or training on the bare walls, only pockmarks.

'Of course.'

'How long – if you don't mind me asking – have you been practising?'

'Practising being sheikh?' The man flung his head back and laughed, revealing some gold teeth.

'Oh, sorry.' Catherine broke out in a blush, the heat crawling up her neck making her itch.

'No practice required, dear one. Born to be sheikh. A gift from father to son.'

She folded her hands in her lap. 'I didn't know.'

'But you brave English woman come for help. No white people ever come.'

'I tried therapy and it didn't work so I thought maybe an alternative method might be... when the boy at the tube station handed me this card... now he gives me one every morning on my way to work. I don't think he recognises me. It's been a few weeks and I have a collection of them.' She rummaged in her purse, pulled out the dozen or so paper-clipped cards and set them on the desk. 'You can reuse these.'

He took them and put them in the drawer. 'My son,' he said, and paused.

'He's the one handing them out for you?'

'Yes. He is fourteen. It keeps him busy from trouble. You like tea?'

Catherine nodded and the sheikh called out an unknown word in a sharp voice. His wife took only seconds to knock and Catherine thought she might have been listening at the door. When he gave his wife permission to enter, she bowed to her husband but kept her gaze on Catherine. When Catherine smiled at her she remained expressionless. The sheikh noticed and said, 'She cooks good and is a beauty too.' He gave her instructions in what Catherine guessed was Arabic and then she backed out of the room, her eyes on the floor. Catherine didn't know what to say. Why had she come here and why was she staying?

'Is that Arabic you were speaking?'

'Yes, of course. But you don't understand.'

Catherine shook her head.

'Arabic should be taught at school. It broadens the mind, opens the heart. With poetry and history mixed in.'

'I never learned another language, but sometimes I watch TV channels – ARTE for French, Al Jazeera for Arabic – and wonder if eventually it'll make sense to me.'

'We can always wonder,' he said.

She wanted to find the right words, to explain what had happened to her family, but she wanted to do it without crying. 'I've tried everything with my aunt. I don't know if I should...?'

'Should what, Catherine?'

'Give up.'

'So you come to Sheikh Abran looking for help.'

She had, but couldn't say why, nor had she told her few friends or colleagues at the library what she was doing. Was it boredom, or desperation or simple curiosity? 'Well, curiosity killed the cat,' she said.

'Who kills cats?'

'No one. It's an expression.'

'OK, fine, but no one kills no one.' He opened the desk drawer and took out a colourless marble the size of his palm and handed it to her. The marble was cool in her hands, and smooth like a river stone.

'Now,' the sheikh said clapping his hands, 'Tell me ten things about Auntie. What you love, what is good with her person.'

Catherine rolled the marble back and forth between her hands, measuring its weight. 'Ten things?'

'Yes.'

'OK. Let's see, she is, oh, I don't know, a very important person. To me.'

'No. You're telling why she is good for *you*, not why she herself is good.'

Catherine looked up at the ceiling, at the paint flaking off in big chunks and the wispy cobwebs in the corner. 'She attracts interesting people in her life.'

'Good, that is a start.' The sheikh's face was calm and open, and he was so still. His face reminded her of a Greek statue she'd seen in a museum with her aunt.

'My aunt is generous. She helps people whenever she can. Only not me. Not anymore.'

'Not a happy situation.'

'No.'

'Continue.'

'Um, she is wise about life. She has a lot of life experience.'

'Her age?'

'Fifty-six.'

'You?'

'Twenty-eight. I celebrated my birthday last month.' Catherine picked up the handkerchief and dabbed at her eyes. Her aunt had not wished her a happy birthday.

'Fortunate wishes for your day of birth.'

'Thank you.'

'Next,' the sheikh said.

'She's my parent. I am an only child. My parents are…' Her chest tightened and she held the handkerchief right up to her face. The lump in her throat pulled so hard it hurt.

'Not in life?' he said in a low voice.

Catherine barely nodded, took a deep breath and removed the handkerchief. The sheikh looked away from her, up at the ceiling, and Catherine looked too, as if there were something else to see.

'What you say is about you, dear one,' the sheikh said, to the ceiling. 'Not about loving Auntie. Must tell six more things about her.'

'I'm not sure I know any more.'

'That is problem: you not know Auntie good enough.'

'Of course I do. I grew up with her.' Catherine squeezed the marble, wanting to crack it open.

The sheikh looked at the windowsill and blew a dead spider away. Catherine took a few deep breaths and they sat in silence for a time, before she felt ready to go on.

'Four: she's steady with people; they can rely on her. Five: she loves her job as a schoolteacher. Six…?'

'Six.'

Catherine shifted and recrossed her legs. Outside the building, on the street below, the newspaper man hollered: '*Evening Standard! Evening Standard!*'

'Catherine, please. Six.' His voice was sharp.

'Let me think.'

'First thing in mind: important.'

'Reena appreciated her life, she was happy with simple things. No great expectations, you know?'

'Reena. Good name.'

'It's unique. Seven: she is good with money. Too good with money.'

'Too good?' He asked. 'Is not possible in London.'

'With her it is. Eight: she lost her husband and doesn't cry about it all the time. She gets on with her life.'

Catherine remembered the funeral and the wake after; how Reena was stacking up empty plastic Tupperware to return to her neighbours. How it was the first time that Catherine had seen Reena accept food from others.

'Nine: she's a great cook.' Catherine brushed her cheeks with the back of her hand. 'And she's very, very sensitive.'

'Like you? She cry easy?'

'I don't cry all that often,' Catherine said, but more tears fell. 'Well, OK: sometimes at night, in the dark. But not every night.'

'You have health problems?'

'I saw my doctor last week.'

'For medicines?'

'Paxil.'

'What is this?'

'It's an antidepressant.'

Sheikh Dr Abran was shaking his head. 'It is a drug. You stop taking.' He leaned over the desk and whispered, 'You have trouble with *juju*?'

'What's that?'

'A spell. The bad spirits take you over and you are no longer you.'

Catherine sat back in her chair thinking about this possibility. Did she believe in magic? Tomorrow at lunchtime she would search for a book on African *juju* in the stacks. 'No, no. It's a medical issue: PTSD. I'm dealing with it,' she blurted out.

He stood up and loomed over the desk. 'Dealing with it?'

She shrank back but then saw he was only shifting the material of his robe around him, which made a poof sound when he sat back down. 'Medicines bad for brain. Bad for heart. Mixing up feeling and thinking.'

Now Catherine stood. 'Listen, I came here for advice on my aunt, not on my health issues. I can't stop taking medication because if I do I won't be able to get out of bed in the morning, I won't be able to go to work, to function. Do you understand?'

'Western medicine: no caring, no understanding. Makes you ill.'

'I don't think this is going to work, with all due respect, Sheikh Dr Abran.' She stood and opened up her wallet. 'How much do I owe you for today?'

'Please sit. I won't say this now. You have the right, please.'

'I'd better get going. I have things to do.' She was holding twenty pounds out when there was a tap on the door.

'Tea time,' the sheikh said. The man's wife entered, carrying a tray with a shiny copper teapot and two brown pottery mugs. The woman looked at them, back and forth before setting the tray down.

'Please sit, I apologise and try harder.' He put his forehead on the desk, as if to pray. The wife nodded at Catherine and gently nudged her to sit also, then lifted the lid off the teapot and wafted minty steam into Catherine's face. She poured a cup for Catherine and set it in front of her. There were fresh mint leaves floating in it.

'Drink your tea,' the sheikh implored. 'Please. We must have patience.'

'OK, but don't—' Catherine said perching on the edge of her seat '—judge me.' She watched as the woman left the room, bowing.

'We go more slowly,' the sheikh told her. 'Bad habits are stubborn.'

'It's not a bad habit; it's a chemical imbalance,' Catherine said in a low voice. 'Do you know what that means?'

'Yes, yes I respect. But let me say: to heal heart we go to the centre of organ, centre of brain. We be kind to self, gentle to you, like gentle to aunt, this solve problem two times. Drink now.'

They sipped their tea in silence. Catherine reread the white cardboard card, which shook in her hands.

SHEIKH DR ABRAN. African Spiritual Healer. Gifted from Almighty God.

She was an atheist, so why had the card captured her? It upset her that she was so desperate as to go into a stranger's house expecting to be convinced of a magical solution. The mint tea opened up her sinuses and made her sniffle and she swallowed the emotion trapped in her throat. Curiosity had always led her astray.

'Please,' he said, passing her another handkerchief from his wooden box.

She dabbed at her sniffly nose and finished her tea.

'Catherine, we work good together. Have patience.' The sheikh smiled showing his large front teeth. 'You come next week, same time?'

Nodding, she said: 'How much do I owe you?'

'No. No money. When problem gone, you pay.'

'But how much will it be? I would like to know.'

'We agree on price when problem solved. We agree. Goodbye, Catherine.'

Now the hall smelled more appealing, like exotic spices frying in oil. She followed the scent and heard the popping of spices in a pan. The kitchen door was ajar and when she peeked in, she saw his wife at the stove with her back to the door.

Catherine scuttled to the front door, calling out 'Goodbye', but not getting an answer.

The next week Catherine went to see the sheikh again after work. This time she walked in bright sunshine, concentrating on keeping her breath even and deep. She thought about what she would say to him, planned how to say it. Up in the third-floor apartment, he was sitting in the same room with the same white robe on; his wife had led her to him once again. Catherine sat without waiting to be asked.

'I think about you. About good aunt. Two good people un-united. Only what you say, understanding missed. Simple problem, simple solution. Please sit and I explain.' The man was nearly bouncing on his chair.

'Why are you in such a good mood?'

'This morning comes with happy news. Client had the break-through and he is joyful. Success is made,' Abran said.

'Oh, right. Do you have a lot of clients, then?'

'Yes, yes. Sheikh Abran have many clients. Catherine want some chai? Mint?'

'Mint would be great – thanks.'

He called out a series of words, which sounded like chopping to her ears, and from somewhere in the apartment came the sound of a small bell rung once, then twice. The sheikh slapped his hands together and Catherine sat up in her chair.

'Copy me,' he said, clapping and rubbing the palms together and she did the same. They continued a dozen more times. 'Now hands on eyes,' he said, laying his hands over his eyes as if to play peekaboo. 'You close eyes. Think on Auntie Reena. She beside you. She say something to you?'

She pressed her palms onto closed eyes and felt warmth like sunshine.

Catherine could picture her aunt easily enough; she had seen into her living-room window from the street just last week. Reena moved more slowly than usual, shuffling across the room to turn on the TV. Catherine squeezed her eyes shut.

'You see Auntie?'

Catherine watched the sparks of light dance under her eyelids, red and orange. She kept them closed and concentrated harder, setting her jaw tight. 'Yes. Yes, I can.' As soon as she said the words, she saw her aunt.

'Tell what she's doing?'

'She's got her yellow rubber gloves on and she's doing the dishes.'

'Imagine she turns now and sees you. What she say?'

'Um? What's she saying?' Catherine peeked out of one eye and noticed the sheikh still had his closed.

'Relax mind, Catherine. Breath deepness in.'

'I think maybe she's asking for help?' Catherine pictured her aunt's pale face and the watery eyes she often dabbed at.

'She in trouble? What she feel? Sad?'

'Yes, I think maybe she's ill.'

'Reena in dis-ease.'

There was a tap on the door and Catherine dropped her palms from her eyes and opened them. The sheikh's reply sounded like scolding. His wife entered, put the tea tray down and quickly left.

'Reena is ill,' he stated.

It could have been her imagination. Or logic. Of course, Reena would still mourn her husband's death. It had only been a year.

'Catherine, serve tea.'

When Catherine poured tea for herself, the man looked at his empty cup and clicked his tongue at her, so she poured him a cup too. A green mint leaf floated to the rim of her cup. She inhaled the scent of mint and honey.

'Mint good for spirit mood. Catherine, you listen. Must call Auntie.' She put her tea down.

'First solution. Simple telephone.'

'I can't. She told me not to call. Ever again.'

'Serious problem. Must be strong. You do things not used to doing, like coming here.'

Two years ago, she'd seen her uncle kissing a woman outside a cinema. He was holding her close to his chest but when his gaze went over the woman's shoulder he caught sight of his niece. Catherine dashed away and walked around for hours, the image replaying of her uncle with his grey beard and thinning hair pulling the blonde woman to him for a tender kiss. Catherine had never seen him embrace her aunt like that.

At first her aunt didn't believe her and told Catherine she was just like her parents, who never liked her choice of men. Catherine denied that, but then it got worse: Reena chose to defend her husband and she refused to speak to Catherine any more – not on the phone or by email or even in person. Catherine's daily attempts tapered off; her aunt was in denial and nothing would bring her to the truth. But then, six months later, her uncle had a heart attack and died. Catherine went to the funeral, thinking that the wall between them would have to come down, but Reena avoided her in the cramped church. Her aunt was busy with the other mourners, but when Catherine went to hug her aunt, to offer support, Reena only tapped her lightly on the back before turning away. Catherine's insides came apart and at home she wept for hours; it was the loneliest place to be, and without her aunt as her anchor she was set adrift. Then, Catherine began to search for help.

After her session, she met his wife at the kitchen door on the way out. The wife was clutching a brown paper bag, which she put into Catherine's hands. It weighed of air. 'What's this?'

'You good girl.' The woman smiled.

Catherine opened the bag and the scent of mint leaves wafted out. 'Thank you. That's very kind.'

The woman rustled in the bag and held up four leaves. 'Hot water, pour over leaves.'

When Catherine moved closer to thank her, the woman backed away and shuffled into her kitchen. '*As-salaam alaikum*,' she said before turning back to the stove.

Catherine did not know how to answer.

Once Catherine was back in her bedsit, she fried a couple of eggs, toasted two slices of white bread and made a pot of mint tea, all the while smelling the spices of the Abran house on her, smells that lingered until she fell asleep.

On her third visit, the sheikh had rearranged his office. The desk was pushed up against the window. 'Better for flow energy,' he said. 'Good light. Look: I read news with sunshine. Good situation.'

Catherine plopped down in her seat. She placed a bag of oranges on his desk. 'These are for you. They're from Spain.'

The sheikh bowed his head and took out an orange, smelled it and sighed. He put the plastic bag on the windowsill where the fruit glowed in the early evening sun.

'So kind. Now, Catherine, tell me news.'

'I called my aunt,' she said. She'd picked up on the fourth ring just as Catherine was about to put the phone down.

'Good! Very good!'

'She hung up on me.'

'Aha, you must go to house. Pack suitcase, tell her you alone, no home. She let in and re-unite.'

He clapped his hands and rubbed them together before laying his palms, as usual, over his eyes. Catherine did the same, feeling the warmth from her hands emanating into her eyelids.

On Saturday morning, Catherine opened the newspaper with her breakfast of tea and toast with marmalade. A headline reported that a 15-year-old North African boy had been stabbed outside the Whitechapel tube station. He'd been swarmed by a gang of kids, who kicked him to the ground and knifed him in the neck – not once but twice. The victim's name was withheld, but the paper reported him in critical condition at the Royal London Hospital. The police called for witnesses to come forward. She had been at that station last night after choir practice but hadn't seen any boys. What if she had talked longer to the choir director and then taken a later train?

She flipped the page to international news and read more about the war in Iraq, which seemed distant and unreal. Catherine sipped her milky tea, knowing that bombs were exploding in the desert, exploding in villages she would never visit. There were photographs of people running and carrying – always carrying – bundles of children, alive or dead.

The next day she bought the Sunday paper. The victim's photo was printed, although he was still in critical condition. He was a black boy with a big smile. The police were holding five suspects.

On Monday, she went for her weekly appointment to the sheikh and had planned on telling him how she had written her aunt a letter and dropped it off by hand. Her aunt wasn't home, though, but she was obviously feeling better because she had pruned her front garden and there were pots of tomato plants on the stoop.

When Catherine reached the third floor and the Abrans' apartment door, it was ajar and she tapped on it, but no one answered and so she walked right in. The usual smells were absent and she hesitated in the hallway; this was the first time she hadn't smelled spices or oil or burnt sugar. When Catherine walked past the kitchen, the sheikh's wife was slumped against the counter holding a handkerchief to her nose. Catherine continued down the long hall with only the sound of her shoes tapping the lino floor.

She knocked on his door but there was no answer and so she pushed it open. The lights in the room were off and the rain had started, strong and sudden, to beat against the window. The sheikh was resting his head on the desk, his small hat beside him. Catherine stood at the doorway and watched his back rise and fall, before he violently shook his head. She stood still, not knowing whether to stay or go and when she whispered his name he didn't respond. Catherine walked in and poured a glass of water from the pitcher on the windowsill and set it down beside him. He looked up and his face was streaked with tears; crescents puffed under his eyes. Catherine stood beside him.

'What's wrong?' she said.

He mumbled and looked out the window.

'Would you like some water?' She pushed the glass towards his elbow but he shook his head and shifted his bare feet under the desk, and moaned.

'What is it?' She said. Everything she had planned to tell him faded from her mind.

His hand pawed at the air, waving her away and so she picked up her bag and, turning back at the door saw him rocking from side to side, speaking under his breath.

'The boy,' he said.

'What boy?' Catherine waited. She looked at the rain-spattered window and listened to the street noises seeping through the thin pane of glass: a screaming child, the *shoosh* of passing cars platooning in puddles, the newspaper man crying, '*Evening Standard!* Get your news!' But it all sounded different today. Catherine entered the room again but stayed at a distance.

'Why? We do nothing for this, why? He was a good boy.'

The newspaper headlines came back: a boy stabbed. 'Is it about what happened at Whitechapel station?'

'Maybe he will die.'

'Did you know the boy?' She poured herself a glass of water.

He shook his head. 'No. My son. My son knows.'

Catherine put her glass down. The son she saw only at the tube station handing out the cards? The son who never seemed to be at home when she arrived?

His wife came in without knocking. She helped her husband to his feet by scooping him up in her thick arms.

'He sleep now. You go.' She steered her husband out of the room, leaving the door open and Catherine stayed in his office for a few moments longer, finishing her water and then looking out of his window. From this height she had a view, through the pouring rain, of the tube station below, and a homeless man outside: a raggedy man, soaking wet, with his hand stretched out. Beside that were the newspaper vendor and a corner shop all within Sheikh Abran's view. How many times did he look out of his window, at the world outside?

Catherine walked down the hall and heard him sobbing from behind his son's door, followed by the soft, appeasing voice of his wife. Catherine was about to leave when she smelled something burning. More wails erupted down the hall and so she pushed open the kitchen door to a billow of smoke mushrooming from a pan of oil. Catherine pulled the pan off the burner, scorching her arm on the gas flame. She flung the pan on the counter and ran her arm under cold water. There was a strange sound – it was the frying pan melting into the counter. She grabbed a dishtowel and moved the pan off the counter and into the sink. Catherine didn't even hear the woman enter the kitchen.

'You!' she screeched. 'Out! Now!'

Catherine kept the cold water running over her arm and stared at the wife.

'My husband upset. You cause upset.' She grabbed on to Catherine's arm but caught sight of the red welt under running water.

'Your pan was burning. It almost set fire to the kitchen,' Catherine said.

The woman turned the water off and bumped Catherine away with her hip. Catherine held up her arm to reveal a pink patch of skin.

'What you my husband say?'

'He's upset about the boy. I'm so sorry. I didn't realise you knew him and I was just trying to help.'

'Please, you go. Too much upset.' The woman pushed Catherine out of the room but held her in the hall while she searched in a drawer. She placed a tube of cream into her hand. 'Go,' was the last thing she said before slamming the door.

She had given Catherine a tube of arnica.

Catherine stood on her aunt's porch, suitcase in hand. It took three long rings on the doorbell before Reena opened the door a crack, saw Catherine and then, ever so gently, shut it again.

'Aunt Reena, I need to speak to you. She heaved her suitcase a step higher. 'Don't leave me standing out here.'

'What is it you want?' The voice was muffled.

'I need to explain something.'

'There's no need,' Reena said.

'Just give me a few minutes?' Catherine said, stifling a cry. 'I miss you.' The door opened a crack and her aunt's face appeared.

'I was kicked out of my flat,' Catherine said.

'Kicked out?'

Reena opened the door a little wider.

'It's just that my roommate's boyfriend moved in,' she said.

'I thought you lived alone in a bedsit.'

Catherine looked down at her aunt's tomato plants; she couldn't think of another argument to offer.

'Are you going to tell more lies, Catherine?'

Catherine shook her head and Reena looked down at Catherine's bandaged arm, at her battered suitcase – the one she'd given to Catherine when she was 16 – now covered in stickers from all the different places her niece had travelled to.

'Still got that old thing?' Reena said. The door was opened wider and Reena's foot came out to nudge the suitcase. Catherine looked up at her with teary eyes.

'You may as well come in now that you're here.'

Catherine went inside but hung back in the hall looking for a tissue in her purse. 'You changed the living room,' she said. It was different shades of pink.

'I overhauled the house last year, got the place redecorated. Salmon suits, don't you think?' Her voice was high and tight.

'It's different. From before, I mean,' Catherine said.

'Got to move on.'

'Yes. Yes, we do.'

'Come in for some tea, and put your case at the bottom of the stairs.'

Catherine sat with her aunt for an hour while her aunt busied herself in the kitchen, baking cookies and tidying up, while avoiding eye contact with her niece. Finally, there was nothing left to do and she washed her hands and sat down at the table. Then Catherine recognised glimmers of the woman she had grown up with, the one who had been her surrogate mother since her parent's accident. Reena's buttercup-coloured kitchen smelled of sugar and yeast. Oatmeal raisin cookies were rising in the oven.

'Bake sale for the church is on tomorrow. You might as well come along and help out if you're going to stick around.' Reena filled her niece's tea cup and stirred milk into it, the way she remembered.

Catherine readjusted the bandage covering the burn. 'I'd like to help.'

Her aunt extended her fleshy hand across the table and took Catherine's. 'What happened to you?' she said, fingering the edge of the bandage.

Catherine's tears, heavy and silent, fell.

'Tell me what you've been up to, girl,' she said and Catherine put her head down on the table and wept loudly and without shame.

The next week, at the usual time of her appointment with the sheikh, no one answered the front bell. She tried to call the number printed on the card, but there was no response, nor was there an answering machine. The next day she dropped by again, this time with flowers. When, again, no one answered, she waited outside until eventually someone came out of the building.

'The bell's not working,' she told him.

'Who are you looking for?' he said.

'Sheikh Dr Abran.'

'Who the bloody hell is that?' he said.

'The African couple on the third floor.'

'Moved out last week, didn't they? Left in a hurry.'

'Can you let me in?'

'Be my guest.' He smirked and let her pass. Catherine took the stairs two at a time and practically fell against the Abrans' door. She knocked loudly but no one opened up. The next-door neighbour came out; he wore a stained undershirt with his hair all mussed up.

'It's no use knocking on that one,' he said.

Catherine noticed a gap in his mouth, a missing front tooth. 'But the Abrans?' she said.

'With the gangster son?'

'Excuse me?'

'His mugshot was in the news, wasn't it? Him and his buddies: little foreign thugs.' The man came closer to Catherine, stood in front of her. The hall lights turned off; they were on a sensor and she moved back and forth to get them to come back on again.

'I don't know what you're talking about,' she said.

His face jutted out, only inches from her, so close that she smelled rancid sweat coming from his wife-beater vest; he was holding a bag of crisps and his breath smelled of bacon.

'Yeah, after his son killed that other kid, the reporters came around, didn't they?'

'Are we talking about the same people? Sheikh Dr Abran?'

'Sheikh? Yah right. I know they've gone cause there's no more stink in the hall. They pissed right off. Probably didn't pay last month's rent.'

'Do you know where they went?'

'I never spoke to 'em. Arab spies, ain't they? Terrorists, I bet. They all are. It's in their blood.'

Catherine felt like she'd been slapped and turned and walked down the hall as fast as she could, praying he wouldn't follow her.

'I got the article here,' he called out. 'Brutal stabbing, victim didn't pull through. Good riddance to bad rubbish, that's what I say.'

She ran down the stairs two at a time, burst out onto the road and looked back up at his dark window. There he was, it was as if she saw him – the sheikh with the palms of his hands covering his eyes – but sitting at a different desk in another room, in another apartment, in a city where anyone could hide anywhere. In a city overwhelmed with people. In a city that shifted and moved like waves in an undefined sea.

Catherine walked over to Whitechapel tube station and waited for the sheikh's son, who handed out those simple paper cards because she didn't believe what the neighbour had told her. She stood by the newspaper kiosk for over an hour, but she never saw him again.

12

Mr Steely, Star-maker

Muriel faces an army of entrance doors, glimmering with brass handles. She plays a guessing game about which one will open for her and leaves fingerprints on the six locked handles. Peering through the bevelled windows into the theatre foyer, there is only darkness.

You took a wrong turn, she scolds herself, but, checking her diary, finds this central London address written down in red ink. Muriel wishes she were back in her dorm room, still sipping tea and reading that novel by P.G. Wodehouse. She imagines being locked away with a hundred of the best novels of the century spread out on her bed. An unlimited supply of Earl Grey. No telephone.

When she turns around to flee home, she notices an alleyway. Taped to the corner of the building is a sign reading 'Auditions: This Way', with an arrow pointing to the side entrance.

This sets off an exuberant cheer, an explosion of goodwill inside her head, where Muriel's most ardent fans live. When she arrives at the stage door there are little mountains of cigarette butts and a shattered champagne bottle. She takes a deep breath and enters.

The abrupt darkness blinds her so that she has to use her hands to guide herself along the wall. Behind her, the door springs shut and the enthusiastic fans in her head abruptly stop cheering.

Why is my support team so highly sensitive?

When her eyes adjust, helped by a small table lamp at the end of the hall, she has the feeling she is being watched by hundreds of eyes. It's the walls. They're plastered with posters of music hall stars from the 1930s: women with bouncy curls and cupid mouths, and men wearing heavy eye make-up. Their cheerful sepia faces fade into the dirty beige wallpaper.

The yawning corridor sucks her in further. When she reaches the end she finds an abandoned reception desk, its wooden top scarred with cigarette burns and coffee-cup rings. Beside the desk is the door to the rehearsal room, dimly lit by a glowing red bulb, the kind seen in old recording studios. *Stop! Do not enter!* it warns. She stands under it, bathed in its warm hue.

Muffled voices escape from the audition room, and when she puts her ear to the door, there's the sound of an actor reciting a classical speech. A second voice, deep and gravelly, interrupts. The actor screams his lines, moving into his upper vocal range, threatening to crack glass.

'Oh ye, herald in the morning!' he screeches.

She imagines his vocal cords springing out of his body like frayed wires. *He's all wrong*, she thinks, backing away from the door. *But who are you to judge?* Muriel's wearing a wrinkled blouse because her iron broke this morning. Thankfully, her feet look great because she spent part of her monthly budget on black patent rehearsal shoes. They are like the ones Dorothy wears in *The Wizard of Oz*, but when Muriel clicks her heels together chanting, 'There's no place like home, there's no place like home,' under her breath, nothing happens.

After a few minutes, the actor on the other side of the wall stops hollering and the silence vibrates in the aftermath. Then there's another sound that she can barely make out. Mice. Clawing at the walls.

She listens to her breath, ragged and irregular. *I will not panic.* She exhales to a count of ten: *One, two, three, four… Relax, relax, relax, and inhale. One, two, three, four.* Dust mites swirl into her nose and a tinny taste surfaces in her mouth. She sneezes just as the auditioning actor begins to sing.

Pulling out a box of tissues, a thermos of hot water with lemon and honey, her allergy pills and a compact mirror from her backpack, she sets down her portable pharmacy on the reception desk. Holding up the mirror, she studies her face from all angles. *Isn't this what you wanted?* She stares at her reflection. 'Who are you, really?' she says aloud and then shoves the mirror back into her bag. Muriel has a problem with boundaries.

But now is not the time for self-analysis (she does enough of that in drama school), it's the time to recite her monologue as Ghislaine from Anouilh's *The Waltz of the Toreadors*. And to practise her character's blocking and gestures: the anguished cry for her lover; the little pistol hidden in her puffy skirt; the swooping faint that will bring Mr Steely to his feet.

Muriel has perfected the subtle intonations, the rising pitch to communicate fragile hope, followed by a drop to show her emotional descent into despair. These are the things she's rehearsed over and over. But the first line of the carefully rehearsed speech escapes her now. She remembers something about wearing a dog collar as if she's someone's pet.

Think, think, think.

She paces up and down the hall, willing the speech to appear fully formed in her brain. She lets her arms dangle at her sides and waits for it. Pinpricks of heat travel through her body and patches of sweat blossom under her arms.

Remember Ghislaine, remember her.

The disturbing thing is that she's already played the character in a drama school production, already repeated this monologue in front of an audience. She acted opposite a 50-year-old student who'd decided late in life to become an actor. The director wanted her to accept kisses from him – on the hands, cheeks and lips, for a total of at least five seconds each time (she'd counted).

'Hold it there... hold it, hold it. Wait – act like you mean it,' the director would say. 'Put your hand on her shoulder, now on her back, now where it counts. Good. Now stroke her hair.'

The fact that she's blanking on the monologue, which she's recited hundreds of times, must mean something. The three-minute piece starts simply enough with the first line, and by remembering that, the rest should bubble up and flow out like a river. But the riverbed is dry and her throat is scratchy, and she's wondering where her cheerleaders have gone, now that she really needs them. Even as she rustles in her bag for the text, she pictures it lying on her bed as she practised in the mirror this morning.

Please come back, sweet, lovely lines.

She's done so much internal work, so many sense-memory exercises.

It's something about wearing a little dog collar around her neck. *Think, think: how does the monologue go?*

The actor inside the audition room screams, then there's the sound of a heavy thud against a wall. Then silence.

A deep wail reverberates in her chest and rushes into her throat, wanting out. No one would hear, except for the sea of glaring eyes on the posters. When she looks at their antiquated faces, she feels their resentment rushing at her. She wants to deface the ringlet-haired Marie Lloyd, music-hall singer circa 1902. Aim a foot at Ella Shields' cherubic smile, with 'Show me the way to go home' printed in gold near her precious face.

'You've had your chance!' she hisses at them, and slumps against the dirty wall, sinking to the tattered carpet. *The dust will infect me, travel through my lungs and choke me to death.* She imagines this happening to her under the watchful eyes of these inanimate witnesses. *I have nothing to give Mr Steely, the star-maker,* she tells them. *I'll make myself disappear.*

Muriel remembers hearing about people who spontaneously combust, leaving only a small mound of ashes behind.

She knows that later on in the green room at drama school, her classmates will act sympathetic. Suzanne will pat Muriel sorrowfully on the back. Secretly, they will all be smiling and she'll have to face her own reflection in the chipped bedroom mirror.

The red bulb above her head flicks off, leaving a shard of white light from the lamp at the end of the hall. Then the studio doors open to spit the boy out, and for a moment, the dirty hall is flooded with light. His long hair is a shroud around his face and as he gets closer, she smells his sweat and sees his eyes wet with something that doesn't look like joy. When the doors close behind him, he reaches out to grab her shoulder and he looks like he's in a state of shock. The boy is breathing heavily and his hand imprints wet heat onto her shoulder. Then he turns away to the side door and escapes into daylight. His image hovers in front of her. His mouth was open as if to give her a message but no words came out of him.

The studio doors fling open again. A disembodied voice calls, 'Next!' and Muriel wades through a deep lake with iron weights on her legs. Multicoloured spots swim in her vision.

The first thing she notices about the audition room is that it's sparse. The floor is of mismatched wooden planks and the walls are covered in pockmarks, as if someone has beaten on them. At the back is a mustard-coloured door with a red EXIT sign above. In the left-hand corner of the room, a stringy-haired man is attached to a piano. In the centre of the studio, where she has stopped, is another man whose snowy head bows over a mountain of photos and CVs. He sits at a folding card table that has one leg askew, and she imagines the whole thing toppling, scattering all of the photos.

This is Mr Steely. She blinks. *Mr Steely, the star-maker.*

The man shuffles through the pile of actors' headshots with his bony fingers. Muriel tries to rearrange her face muscles into a smile but he doesn't look up. As he flips through the images looking for hers, she catches fragments of eyes and teeth. In the corner, the pianist stares at his hands, a cigarette dangling between his lips, the corners of his mouth weighed down by gravity. No one says hello.

Am I really here? Or still trapped in the dark hallway? If they don't notice me within 30 seconds will I be absorbed by the floorboards and declared missing?

Someone once explained astral projection to her and she wonders if this is it: the yawning hallway, the red light bulb, the anonymous boy holding on to her shoulder.

If I'm not really here then I won't have to sing for them. A natural smile forms on her lips and she feels her feet firmly planted, steady for once.

'Hello Miriam,' the casting director says. His body is still bent over the card table.

Maybe he has a spinal injury and can't lift his head? 'Muriel, actually,' she says.

When he looks up, his gaze takes her in, from head to foot. She's been told not to look directly into his eyes, but they are magnetic. They have a moment, a showdown.

Either he's going to obliterate me or I'll drown in those glacial blue eyes.

Lines crossing lines mark his loose skin; he has the face of a West End theatre battlefield. His white hair is like angel hair strewn on a Christmas tree. He lifts a shaky wrist to check his watch, and then taps on the table.

'I take it we have your CV, young lady?' He coughs and a rattle vibrates inside his chest.

'Yes, I did send it – but, but I have another one here if you like.' She can't stop her head from bobbing: nod, nod, nod. *Control yourself!* The nodding continues. *You're making a scene! Oh God!* (She's not a religious person except in auditions.)

Shifting through a smaller pile of photos on the makeshift table, he lands on hers. Holding up the eight-by-ten glossy, he looks her up and down, then at the photo and then back at her. She wants to prostrate herself, cradle his gnarled feet.

'Give Shaun your sheet music,' he says.

Muriel forces herself across the room to hold out the score for Irving Berlin's 'Be Careful It's My Heart'. The pianist exhales violently from his cigarette when he takes it.

'I assume you're here for *Les Mis*,' Mr Steely says.

'Um, actually it was for *The Phantom, The Phantom of the*—'

The pianist looks over at Mr Steely.

'Yes, Shaun, we'll do the song first,' the director says.

Muriel has backed up to what she thinks is the centre of the room, although she's tempted to get the ruler out of her backpack and measure. *Perfection comes from within,* she reminds herself.

'Whenever you're ready.' He folds his hands over her photo and her heart explodes into little tremors. As soon as she clears her throat her singing teacher's voice rings out in her head: 'Never clear your throat before singing. It sounds amateurish.' Taking a deep breath, she nods at the pianist, whose first note hammers through the heavy air. Muriel opens her mouth wide like a hungry bird.

'Sweeeeeetheaaaart of miiine, III've sent youuu a valentiiine…' her voice escapes in a crooning Patsy Cline way. She shouldn't have listened to *Cline's Greatest Hits* last night.

Think: think fast!

She was taught in singing class to use imagery to bring the song to life, to make it her own, so she envisions singing it to the love of her life. He'd be a cross between Brad Pitt and Johnny Depp. He'd have Johnny's pout and Brad's blue, blue eyes. Although she's merged their faces in the best-possible way, she draws a blank when she tries to visualise what their baby would look like and whose genes would dominate. This is a problem she'll have to solve later. She turns her thoughts to Canada and the boyfriend she left behind.

'Sweetheart of mine, it's more than a Valentine…'

The image of her London boyfriend pops up and blocks out the Canadian guy. She feels obliged to sing to him, even though they've been arguing far too much lately because he wants her to cook dinner every night *and* do the dishes after a long day at drama school. She hits the wrong note and is jolted back into the studio.

Whatever you do, don't look at the star-maker. Look above his head, just slightly.

She forces herself to concentrate on the piano notes rising and mingling, but a fly is buzzing around her in a square formation. It lands on the red exit sign over the door at the back of the room high above Mr Steely's head. Muriel sings to the fly, giving it her full, unadulterated passion.

When she finishes, she stands still, but then becomes overly aware of her dangling arms, which have never seemed longer, while the last piano note merges into the sound of Mr Steely scribbling on a notepad. She can only wait, wait and wait. *Breathe in: one, two, three. Out: three, two, one.* The fly dive-bombs Mr Steely's card table. The pianist's cigarette smoke drifts in an elegant line towards her.

She counts to 20 in her head while he continues to scribble. She wants to run to the flimsy card table, grab the paper out of his tobacco-stained fingers and demand that she get the part. Instead, she concentrates on keeping still.

When he looks up, he raises his furry eyebrows.

'And your monologue is?'

She licks her lips and tries out her Mona Lisa smile. Her cheerleaders are whooping for joy. She imagines herself as a courtesan, her head tilted gracefully to the side, a purple cigarillo in a golden holder balanced between dainty fingers.

'Ghislaine, from *The Waltz of the Toreadors*. I played Ghislaine at drama school, in a production of *The Waltz of the Toreadors*, where I was the lead. She's the heroine of *The Waltz of the Toreadors*. In the play that I just mentioned.'

Sirens squeal in her head. There's an echo in the room: *Ghislaine, Ghislaine, Ghislaine.* The two men look at each other, back at her, then at each other again while Muriel bows, turns a slow circle in incantation, and by the time she's facing them again the monologue returns, whole and floating in her head. Her lines were only frightened animals hiding in the cave of her mouth, and she merely had to coax them out. The speech starts strong because she throws herself into it and speaks it like music: all cadence and breath. Then in the best part, when Ghislaine pleads to her hero, Gaston, just before the carefully choreographed swoon, Mr Steely interrupts.

'Thank you.'

The image of her hero morphs into the West End star-maker, who grins for the first time, his eyes closing for a quick second like a double wink, and she quickly forgives him his rudeness, his power, his rumoured preference for boys.

'Mirima, we'll be in touch,' he tells her.

'Muriel. My name is Muriel.' She thanks the two men, although she can't see the pianist through the haze of his own smoke. She escorts herself out by walking backwards and half-bowing, Japanese-like.

After closing the studio door, Muriel looks up to see if the red light had been on for her but it's dark. She had expected to find another actress waiting, but she's alone. She stays still until her eyes readjust to the diffused light. The lamp at the end shines at her like a beacon. Running her fingers over the weathered reception desk, she traces the circular stains in the wood. She was angry at them before but now she gazes up at the poster of Ella Shields, ringletted and demure and whispers to them, 'I'm going home now.' Muriel glides along the ancient carpet and runs her hands along the dusty wallpaper, removing some of its history and taking it outside with her.

The dazzling sun reflects off shop windows and splashes silver diamonds on people's faces. Muriel escapes the shadow of the theatre and moves into the sunshine, merging with the stream of pedestrians. Catching her reflection in a tobacco shop window, she is all golden, as if she is under the brightest spotlight and the star-maker's double wink is still fresh in her mind.

PART IV

Hawaii

13

Poisonwood Gods

Broken shells swirl in the water around her legs and the undertow tugs like a needy child. Sarah leans away from the drop-off point, not daring to go further where the undertow would sweep her out to open sea. Her husband splashes water on his head and it streams down his face in sheets; the sun glints on his teeth through the water as if liquid sunshine were radiating from his mouth. They're on the eastern tip of the island of Molokai, Hawaii, between the rumbling Pacific and the serene Halawa Valley, a formation over a million years old. Velvety folds of green and brown mountains rise up behind them as a testament to evolution, but she has been feeling uneasy for the past hour.

'Time to go,' she says, planting her feet one after the other in the soft sand. Stephen runs behind, shaking his head to tease water from his curls. They wander up the beach to their dusty rental car, parked at the end of a dirt road leading back into the rainforest. When tiptoeing over prickles and dry twigs, Sarah steps on something sharp and cries out and Stephen scoops her up in his arms. She closes her eyes and, with his hot breath on her face, imagines that they're approaching the altar to get married again. Instead, Stephen plants her down beside the car, near squat trees with shredded, wiry branches.

In the vehicle, grains of black sand grind in their bathing suits. Her towel falls off her shoulders and Stephen lowers her bathing-suit strap and kisses her in the hollow. She grabs his wet head with both her hands and joins her mouth to his; they dance their tongues around in a briny kiss until he pulls away. A curl of hair sticks to his forehead and she wipes it away.

'Let's go back to the hotel,' he says. She lifts and kisses his palm so delicately that he has to adjust himself in his bathing suit before putting the key in the ignition. When he turns the key, nothing happens. On the next try, he applies force but there's only a clicking sound. Stephen stares at the dashboard, stunned. Sarah stares at him. He tries five more times as if it's only a matter of time.

'Let me try,' she says but he brushes her hand away.

'It's not going to make a difference who turns it.'

Sarah looks out the window up at the twisting coastal road.

It had taken an hour and a half to get to this deserted beach miles from their vacation rental. Situated at the end of a lonely route across the island, it ribboned over the crest of the Halawa Valley. They had veered around rock cliffs before descending down a craggy mountainside.

'There used to be sacred fishponds in the area,' she had told Stephen while they were driving down to the cove, gazing at the cliff face and into the Pacific Ocean.

'It's a good thing one of us read the guidebook,' he'd said. At the time he had been smiling at her. Sarah had stroked the back of his head while he kept his eyes fixed on the snaky road, always a cautious driver.

'Now there's just this black sand beach – if we can ever find it,' she'd said.

'I can't believe this is the only safe place to swim. After all the tourist pictures you see, can the island be that treacherous? I mean, really?' he'd replied. He had taken his eyes off the road for a quick second to smile at her. Then they had been silent, amazed at the ear-popping descent as they veered down to get to the hidden cove at the tip of the island. But that was hours ago.

The stale air in the car forces Sarah to roll down her window, and she breathes in, listens. 'Do you hear that?' she asks. Wild dogs are barking in the distance. She guesses they might be behind the low-lying brush on the far side of the beach. Just this morning, she'd read the warning in the guidebook: *Wild dogs travel in packs and are often starving. We recommended keeping your distance.*

'Wild dogs are the roaming spirits of lost souls,' she says, but Stephen has disappeared under the dashboard. 'Do you hear them?'

He only grunts as he tries to hotwire the car. Since the wedding they've been spending more uninterrupted time together than ever before and she's still discovering the limits of his patience – patience being like two thin walls easily blown down.

He pops the hood of the car and gets out; she follows him. He burns his hand on the sun-infused metal and, without so much as a whimper, sticks his head under the hood. Sarah watches his narrow back, at the slender muscles pulling beneath his T-shirt. When he comes up for air, he mops his forehead with long, piano-playing fingers and looks mesmerised. They stare down at the inner workings of their rental car while the light on the mountains deepens to a greyish purple. Stephen finds the cell phone and tries it.

'There's no reception.'

'Maybe we're too far down in the valley? I didn't see a phone box along the road, did you?' Further up the beach, she sees tiny moving dots, but not human. 'Look at that,' she points. 'The dogs are coming.'

He looks at where she's pointing. 'Wait in the car.'

There's a greasy bag of macadamia nuts in the glove compartment. She counts out four for him, and five for herself then pops hers, one by one, into her mouth. She takes a swig of the bottled water and discovers it's at just the right temperature for a cup of tea.

The guidebook describes the legend of Molokai as an island of sorcery called *po'oko'i* in the Hawaiian language. Here, there were evil deities and altars for human sacrifice. The Poisonwood Gods or *Kalaipahoa* came in the 16th century and were believed to inhabit trees and suck the life from them. When the local woodchoppers tried to cut down the forest, they were killed by the infected leaves and branches. The curse was so potent that even passing birds fell to their deaths. Sarah decides they'll starve before they touch a coconut tree.

Her grandmother had believed in curses and revealed them to Sarah at an early age. Once, she put one on a nosy neighbour, a peeping

Tom. The man's petunias wilted and he blamed her grandmother's dog for peeing on them, but he also stopped looking in Sarah's bedroom window at night. Her grandmother told Sarah that a murdered person will haunt the earth forever. Sarah wishes she could find out what happens to a person who dies from something slower, like hunger or heatstroke. But it's too late to ask because her grandmother has left the world.

When Sarah has finished her nuts she pops one of Stephen's into her mouth, rolls it around on her tongue, and sucks off the salt before crunching down. In the 19th century, the fear of Molokai as a place of evil is what protected the island from being invaded. She claps the book shut; this is their vacation, after all, but Sarah can't help but imagine the article in the newspaper back home: *Honeymooners perish on the dangerous cape of a cursed Hawaiian island.* Would anyone find their bodies?

Stephen slams down the hood with unusual force and it jerks her out of her daydream. He reaches into the glove compartment and pulls out a Mars bar, taking a bite before offering it to Sarah. The warm, gooey chocolate coats her teeth with a ribbon of caramel and she smiles at him. But after only one bite, he grabs the bar back and hurls it towards the bushes, far from them, where it lands in the sand.

'Hey,' she says and gets out of the car to pick it up. 'What was that for?'

'Leave it for the dogs. It'll keep them off our trail.' He pockets the keys and walks away. 'Stay in the car,' he calls back. 'I'll see if there's anyone up the road.'

She watches him go for two seconds and then follows, running after, trying to keep up with his long gait as they enter the forest. She imagines they're the couple from *Romancing the Stone* who hack through the jungle, swing on vines and scale rocky cliffs.

'I told you to stay behind.'

'But the dogs,' she says.

'Did you lock the doors?'

She decides not to answer and he lets it go. They continue up the narrow forest path illuminated by the rays of sunshine, which laser through gaps in the foliage. Some of the leaves look like long swords, and others have the almond shape of eyes; all of them shift in the breeze. The swords scythe and scratch. The small leaves shush and flutter. Stalks of green bananas cling to the trees. When she tries to count the fruit, she's distracted by a phallic-looking object dangling from the bottom of the cluster. The purple flower, shaped like a teardrop, is the size of her outstretched hand. At the bottom of the flower drips a clear gooey fluid and although she's tempted to touch it, it's too high above her head. Besides, it could be poisonous. She lures her husband back to show him this miracle of nature.

'We have to get out of here before dark,' he says without stopping.

Sarah jogs to keep up with his stride and concentrates on the crunching of branches underfoot. Some of these leaves are as large as her body. Further up the trail, a white clapboard church rises out of the forest's green palette and the feeling of gratitude at seeing something man-made surprises her. It's as if they've been lost for days. As they near it, they see its state of disrepair: the chipped paint shingles and the faded red roof. Stephen pushes the wooden door open.

'We can sleep here if we need to,' he says, ducking under a spiderweb.

Sarah follows him. Inside, a light beam streams through a crack in the window and lands on the altar. Spider-webs stretch across the aisles of wooden pews and the stone tiles are scattered with dried banana leaves. Jesus, fixed to the altar, is small and white and stares at the floor. Stephen stays near the entrance while Sarah walks up to the altar.

'I wish I'd been brought up with a belief in you, but my parents were atheists,' she whispers to the miniature Jesus.

'Hey, Stephen,' she calls out looking back for him, but he's gone already. Sarah gently closes the door and finds him on the path, waiting for her.

'Stephen, I know a prayer that grandma taught me. Do you know the St Christopher one?'

He shrugs.

'It's for travellers.'

'Never heard of it,' he says, ushering her ahead of him.

'Grant me a steady hand and watchful eye. That no one shall be hurt as I pass by.' Her voice drifts up into the trees. 'Then something – about a car I think.' They continue in silence, while the sounds of the rainforest reverberate: trilling birds, buzzing insects, rustling fronds that scrape against each other like grasshoppers' legs.

'Teach me to use my car for need, nor miss through love of undue speed, the beauty of the world.'

Stephen stops and turns to her, cradles her face in his hands, kisses her and then breaks away to race ahead. She has to catch her breath before she moves on. After about 10 minutes of walking, they hear a barking dog and a gruff male voice scolding someone. Stephen parts the overgrown branches to reveal a family of *kanaka* which, according to her guidebook, are people of native Hawaiian ancestry. Two men, a woman, and two children pile into a white pickup truck with a motorboat hooked on the back. Stephen drops the branches to hide him and Sarah, but she pushes him forward so that they stumble into the glade and face the truck. The group look up and peer at them from behind the murky windshield. A black dog stands on alert in the motorboat behind them.

The couple approach the driver who steps out of the vehicle, shirtless and as wide as the two of them put together. Stephen grabs her hand. 'Our car. It won't start,' he says, pointing through the bushes. 'It's stuck back there.'

The man smiles. 'Oh yeah? That's bad luck.'

Stephen nods. 'You could call it that.'

The Hawaiian man looks at them, and then turns to leave. On his broad back is a tattoo of a massive turtle. 'We gotta get round the north side you know, before dark. Get this boat in the water,' he says.

Sarah steps around Stephen but he holds her back.

'Well, is there anyone else around who could help us?' Stephen says.

'No idea. You know, people don't live on this side, heh? Not for tourists.' The man looks at Sarah, scans her.

'We just need a boost. Could you? It'll just take – I don't know – a minute?' Stephen rifles in his wallet and approaches the truck, holding out a fifty in his trembling hand. The Hawaiian looks at the money and shrugs his shiny, brown shoulders. 'Hey buddy, the weather's going to turn, like I said. We've got to take off.'

'Maybe you have a phone we could use so we could call a tow truck.'

'There's no signal down here,' he says.

'But what are we supposed to do? We're down there at that beach.'

The man turns back to them, takes a step forward. His brown eyes narrow. 'You're at the cove?'

Sarah nods. 'At the black sand beach,' she says.

The Hawaiian grasps an amulet he wears around his neck. 'You went down to the cove?' he repeats and looks at them as if they've just killed someone. 'Who told you about it?' The kids are getting restless in the truck, but the Hawaiian doesn't break his gaze. Sarah sinks to her knees onto branches and leaves. The sky's light is fading. She listens to the shushing of the trees. Drops of sweat run down the man's bare chest and into his belly button. She imagines they're captured in a photo; she looks up at the hazy sky while the Hawaiian stares, Stephen looks down at her, and the four passengers peer out of their truck. It is so quiet – an envelope of silence is padding them. When the Hawaiian leans through the truck window and whispers to his passengers, Sarah tries to catch her husband's eye. The dog jumps out of the boat, lopes over to Sarah and promptly smells her crotch.

'They're our only chance,' she tells Stephen as she gets up to go to the truck.

The man gets into his vehicle, slams the door and rolls down his window. 'You know, there's got to be someone else around,' he says.

Stephen hangs back while Sarah looks inside the truck. 'We were alone down there,' she says.

One child, a girl of five or so, plays peek-a-boo through the dirt-streaked window. The boy looks a couple of years older; he's drinking Coke from a family-sized bottle. The Hawaiian starts his engine and Sarah steps away.

'Wait!' Stephen calls out but the vehicle moves forward, crushing leaves under its weight and Stephen runs towards it.

'Please!' he yells, but the driver revs up and disappears through the trees. 'Jesus Christ!'

Stephen kicks at the dry earth. Sarah walks away from the trail and the dog follows, looking at her with wet eyes. His black back is jumping with dust and fleas. Then, from behind the bush, they hear the man crying: 'Dodge! Dodge, get over here!' The animal's ears prick up but he stays still.

'Dodge,' she whispers pointing at the forest, 'go back to your owner.' He rubs up to her, leaning against her legs with his scratchy fur on her bare skin. 'You want to stay with us?' He whines when she pets him behind the ears. 'He wants to stay,' she says.

When the truck backs up through the trees, the man calls, 'Dodge, get your ass over here!' But the dog lowers his head and doesn't move. It's only when Sarah walks over to the truck that he follows. When she reaches the idling vehicle, she looks the man in the eye and says, 'If you want your dog back, you'll have to take us too.' The kids stop playing peek-a-boo.

'I told you, we can't,' he says. His words come out like punches.

She rests her hand on his windowsill. 'Come on. You can't leave us stranded here. We're tourists. What if we die of starvation or something? Or the wild dogs get us.'

The man looks over to his buddy, who is sitting in the middle.

'It'll take us days to walk back to town. Plus it's getting dark,' Sarah says. 'We could be hit by a car.' Her back is slippery with sweat. 'When you read about us in the paper, you'll have to live with the guilt, knowing you could have helped but didn't. Your kids,' Sarah says, bending over to look at the girl and boy in the back seat, 'they won't forget us.' The children stare at her with their wide, dark eyes. 'Will you?' she asks them directly. 'I'm Sarah and that's Stephen, my new husband.'

The Hawaiian looks down at Dodge. 'Fine,' he says. 'Get in the boat and we'll go to the cove.'

'Thanks,' she says, 'we really appreciate it.'

'Just get in,' he says.

She motions to Stephen before scrambling into the boat and he joins her. Dodge does a flying leap after them and falls over when his claws hit the slippery bottom. Saliva drips out of his gummy mouth and onto her knees and he licks her bare legs, and she lets him.

'What did you say to convince him?' Stephen asks, but she only squeezes his hand. They sit side by side, riding over rough terrain.

The boat teeters sideways, so they hold onto the sides and duck under low tree branches. The kids knock on the rear window and give them the hang-loose sign, a gesture she's seen in surfing movies. On the forest path, they're dappled with weak rays of sunlight streaming through the trees; ribbons of light play across their faces. When they pass the banana trees, she points out the sexy maroon flower. The driver turns toward the beach and their car, now immersed in shadow.

'This cove is a sacred ritual ground,' he yells back at them through the open window 'It's not for tourists.' The kids' eyes turn wide and serious as they stare through the truck window at Sarah and Stephen. 'How did you escape the Poisonwood Gods?' he calls back and his male friend laughs in a way that cuts the air in two. When they reach the cove he stops the truck beside their car but his passengers stay in their seats. 'Get out of the boat,' he tells them. Dodge leaps out first and the Hawaiian leashes him with a dirty rope to the bumper of the truck. Stephen takes the keys out of his pocket and walks to the car. The shirtless man follows and Sarah watches as her husband hands over their car keys and the man pockets them.

'OK now. You guy, take off your shirt,' he tells Stephen.

Stephen straightens and looks at the burly man. 'Why?'

The man looks at Sarah and says, 'You too.' Dodge barks and wags his tail. She wonders if her bathing suit is visible under her T-shirt, then it wouldn't be so bad.

'Just do what I say.'

She lifts the shirt over her head, to reveal a damp yellow bikini top, the one she bought on sale back home. Stephen takes a long time removing his UC Berkeley T-shirt.

'Now the bottoms,' the Hawaiian says, looking out at the ocean. Sarah turns to her husband but he stands still in the sand, his head cocked to the side, his brow furrowed. She can see his jaw pulsating. Dodge strains at his leash, whimpering.

'What for?' Stephen says.

The Hawaiian looks back, his brown eyes unwavering.

'It's the car, remember? Stalled there. We need you to look at the engine,' Stephen says. 'Or give us a boost.'

'Please,' Sarah begs.

The Hawaiian turns away, pushing at the sand with his foot, and Sarah looks at his tattoo – the faded inky turtle stretched across his broad back. When he turns, he says 'Strip down,' and his mouth is twisted up in a way that makes them do it. The other people watch through the truck windows.

'Now,' the man points to the ocean. 'Go down to the water.'

Sarah finally understands; he isn't just going to rob them. She looks at the dirty brown sand covering the yellow flip flops she bought. To match her new bathing suit. For their honeymoon.

'Stephen?' she whispers, but he won't answer. 'What do we do?' She crosses her arms across her breasts. He puts his arm around her shoulders. A wind blows across their naked bodies.

'Go on, get down to the water,' the Hawaiian says in a flat voice. The male friend gets out of the truck and leans against it, playing with a lighter. He flicks it on each time the little flame is blown out by the breeze.

Stephen looks at her but speaks to the Hawaiian: 'I don't know what you want but—'

The man opens a wide mouth full of child-sized teeth and yawns. He stares at the ocean and waits. Sarah listens to the cacophony of sound: rustling trees, pounding waves, barking dog, and her own pulse flooding her ears. Lepers were banished to this island for over a hundred years – she read that they were brought here from all the Hawaiian islands and thrown from boats into the shallow waters to sink or swim, their open wounds exposed to painful, salty water. Legally declared dead by their own government.

Taking Stephen's sweaty hand, she pulls him towards the shore. She doesn't think they've ever been naked in public; at least she hasn't. The dog's bark is short and staccato. Though the wild dogs aren't visible, the Mars bar has disappeared from the sand near the car. She racks her brain for an idea, an escape.

When they reach the shore, and look out at the expansive horizon, he calls out, 'OK, now hold your hands above your head.'

This is it! Sarah thinks. She squeezes Stephen's hand with all the force in her. She knows Stephen has a hundred dollars in his wallet, in his shorts, back up on the beach. She could tell the man to look in there, but she can't make her mouth move. She'll throw herself in front of Stephen to absorb the bullet. She wonders if her life will flash in front of her eyes, like they tell you it does. Will her grandmother be waiting for her?

Their hands are sweating as if they're holding hot coal between them. Then her knees release and Stephen pulls her back to him, bracing her to his side.

'It's OK,' he says. 'It's going to be OK.'

She hears a distant whoosh of water reverberating in her ears – the dull thud of her heart pumping blood into her head.

'Do what I said.'

'Goodbye, love,' she whispers, putting her hands up in the air. But nothing happens. When Stephen and Sarah turn around, the Hawaiian is staring at them. His arms stretch forward, hands curved up as if he's holding two enormous bowls in front of his chest.

'Makai,' he says simply. 'Turn and face the water.'

She spins around and Stephen follows.

'Look at the horizon.'

They do. They also steal glances at each other, eyes filled with love, regret, sorrow.

'Now, kneel down in the water. Put your hands in the water.'

She thinks of how she started swimming at six when her dad threw her in the deep end.

'Get way down.'

How the water got into her nostrils and she thought her brain was swimming. All at once, it makes sense: drowning, that's his method. There'll be no evidence. The undertow will sweep them away like driftwood, out to the open sea. She kneels until the water covers her sunburned thighs. But they are still at the shore, not yet close to where she'd felt the undertow. Stephen says something she can't hear.

'Now,' the Hawaiian says, 'put your noses to the water.'

She wants to tell the man that they were married in California last week, in a garden by the beach with over a hundred family members and friends. Her bouquet was yellow freesias. Yellow is the colour of hope. Their photos are being developed right now. She rehearses what she could say. When she looks over her shoulder, the other

Hawaiians are there too, standing beside the friend, who is still flicking his lighter on and off.

'Keep your eyes on the water. Now lean down and smell that ocean,' he tells them. 'Put your noses in it, get right in there.'

She leans over the surface of the water and inhales salty brine. Droplets spray her face. Stephen sneezes water out of his nose, and jumps up yelling. 'That's enough. What are you trying to prove?' But he loses his footing and falls back down into the sand. Sarah pulls him gently back to kneeling beside her and grasps his hand under the opaque water. The sharp edges of jagged shells cut her sunburned knees.

'We're good swimmers,' she whispers. 'We could make it around the cove, on the left side there.' Along the horizon is a tanker.

'*Haole*,' the Hawaiian calls, and something clicks in Sarah's mind. '*Haole*,' he repeats. '*Haole. Haole. Haole.*'

The word. She'd read it in the guidebook. She turns back to look at the man; he's chanting with eyes closed; he sways. He lifts his arms to the sky. His friends are staring at him too.

'Foreigners,' she says and squeezes Stephen's hand with its pruney fingers. 'That's what it means.'

'Repeat after me,' the Hawaiian says, breaking into a series of words she can't understand. He walks down the beach to them. '*Honua. Honua.*'

The couple repeat the sound but he changes it.

'*Aikane. Aikane.*'

They repeat this word.

The Hawaiian comes closer, now standing behind them. '*Honua. Honua,*' he chants to the sand. '*Kokua. Kokua,*' he speaks to the sky. '*Malihini. Malihini,*' he says to them. Then his arms swoop over their heads toward the ocean, to the mountains and the sky. In a booming voice he calls out, '*Mahalo. Mahalo.* Repeat.'

Sarah cries, '*Mahalo! Mahalo!*' And Stephen follows, his deep voice underscoring her trembling one. The three of them call out the word together. '*Mahalo.*' It feels soft and round, like turning over a warm stone on her tongue.

'Now put your hands on the surface of the water.' The man comes down to the shore and into the water. He stands beside her and puts his own palms face down on the little choppy waves.

'*Mahalo. Mahalo.*'

Sarah's eyes drop, fatigue drags her down.

'Now stand up in the water.'

Sarah's skin is mottled with goosebumps.

'Now turn around and look at the mountains. Greet them: *Mauka.*'

She can't see much definition on the mountains anymore because the light is dusky; only the faint wavy lines of the folding valley appear. There's something hypnotic about his voice, like honey coating rough sand.

'Now turn around and let your eyes follow the horizon. Now again: *Mahalo, Mahalo.* Repeat and turn: *Mahalo, Mahalo.* Repeat and turn.'

They must have said the word 20 times already. When she turns, she sees Stephen's pulse vibrating in his neck. The water laps at their legs. She is shivering.

The little girl sings a song, different but complementary, her voice filling the air. The Hawaiian goes silent and she continues sweetly, dissolving on the last note. Two birds fly out of a nearby banana tree over their heads, then away from them and into the dusky Halawa Mountains.

'OK,' the man says. 'Come out of the water now.'

She looks into the Hawaiian man's brilliant face. He's fingering a carved bone hanging on a thin string around his neck.

'It's your lucky day,' he explains pointedly, as if speaking to children. 'I've cleared you of any bad spells. Your car too.'

Stephen looks as though he just woke up from a slumber.

'You understand, guy?' He smiles at Stephen flashing his little teeth. 'You are clear and free to go.'

His friend with the lighter laughs and it sounds like a minor explosion, jolting them out of their half-state. 'You bastard!' the friend says, slapping the Hawaiian on the back. The woman stands beside the truck and speaks in a flat tone. 'Ha, ha,' she says, 'playing with the tourists again.' She walks over to the little girl, who is dancing her doll in the sand and takes her hand, leading her back to the vehicle. The Hawaiian waits for Stephen and Sarah by their rental.

'Now let's get your hunk-a-junk started and we can be on our way.'

The three of them head up the beach and the man's friend sidles up to Stephen.

'Kvai,' the friend says nodding toward the big Hawaiian, 'is from a Kahuna family.'

Stephen looks at him blankly.

'You know *Kahuna*?'

The man tries with Sarah, but she shakes her head.

'That was a *mele*-like thing. An ancient chant.'

'Really?' Sarah says.

'Kahuna is like a Hawaiian priest, like from an old lineage, you get it?' he tells them. 'See the thing around his neck. That's the symbol for a Kahuna family.'

Sarah nods but Stephen doesn't bother looking. They stop when they reach Kvai, leaning up against their car door. 'Hey Kvai, show them your amulet, man.'

He has spread out their wet clothes on the hot hood of the car. 'Here's your keys. It's good to go now,' he says, rapping on the hood.

Sarah takes the keys and gives them to her husband. 'We think it's the battery,' she tells Kvai, putting her wet bathing suit back on and getting her fingers stuck in the pockets of her shorts. 'I guess it needs a jump-start.'

She dumps Stephen's clothes into his arms, nudging him to dress, but there's something slowed-down about her husband and his eyes are blurry.

Kvai shakes his head. 'No, no. I mean the car's good to go *now*. Try it.'

The Hawaiian man joins the woman and kids by the truck and hustles them in. The friend follows while Sarah and Stephen watch them all pile into their vehicle, slamming the doors and starting the engine.

Sarah gets into the driver's seat, puts the key in, turns it and hears the catch of the ignition. Stephen leans down and stares at her through the window. 'But how could – what did he do?'

Sarah gets back out and they stare at the family in the truck and Dodge in the boat. Kvai's massive arm rests on the windowsill.

'Got to go!' he yells. 'The daylight, you know.' The sky has turned mauve. 'Going, going, gone.' He flashes a huge smile.

Sarah looks up at the sky, feeling as if she just dropped out of a parachute.

'You are a blessed couple you know, being here, getting a taste of our *mana*.' He holds an arm out the window and gestures to the rainforest, the sea, the sky. 'It's spiritual power, man.'

The kids squeal in the back seat.

'This is real-live Hawaii, my friends! *Nei!* Beloved Hawaii!' he yells up to the sky. 'Just be careful not to disrespect the Poisonwood Gods, yeah?' He nods to them. 'And hey, follow me out of here and quick too.'

The truck pulls out of the sand and crawls up the long path to the rainforest. Dodge whimpers, his eyes still set on Sarah. Stephen gets into their car, but Sarah doesn't move from her spot on the beach, she just watches them drive away. There are many words to show gratitude in the Hawaiian language, but she can't remember any, so she calls out the simple word that means love, hello, and goodbye all in one. 'Aloha!' she cries. 'Aloha!' When she gets in the car she turns to her husband.

'Can you believe that?'

The car battery hums quietly. Stephen looks back at her frowning. 'The battery needed a rest, that's all,' he says.

'What? No, that's not it.' Patches of heat rise up her neck. 'Don't you believe that he…? Stephen?'

Her husband doesn't answer, only opens his window and steps on the accelerator. They follow the truck, inching up the forest path before leaving the forest for the winding single-lane road, which curves around the steep cliffs overlooking the Pacific. Now the sun is shining only a finger of light above water; darkness is closing around them.

Sarah stares down at the dark churning sea. 'He saved us,' she whispers.

On Stephen's side are ragged cliff walls framing roughly cut patterns in the rocks, which before their very eyes become shadowy masses in the fading light. Sarah pushes a button to open all the windows in their car so they are blown about by sea air. Stephen's gaze is fixed on the red tail-lights of Kvai's truck but he keeps a large distance between the vehicles.

Sarah rests her hand on her husband's thigh and they're silent all the way back to the hotel, but when they get there they strip off their sun-kissed clothing and make love with their newly blessed bodies.

Publications

'Candyman', *1097Mag,* 2007, online

'Candyman', *Pharos Literary Magazine,* British Institute, Paris, France, 2004

'Infertile Land', *Menda City Review,* Iss. 28, California, USA, 2016

'Lost Time' *Tinge Magazine,* Iss. 11, Philadelphia, USA, Spring 2016

'Love Bites', *Penmen Review,* Southern New Hampshire University, USA, July 2015

'Love Bites', *The Bitter Oleander: A Journal of Contemporary International Poetry & Short Fiction,* Vol. 21, No. 2, New York, USA, Autumn 2015

'Phantom Appendage', *decomP magazinE,* Ohio, USA, 2015

'Sunday in the Park with Betty', *Dachkammerflimmern, Hamburg Writers Room Anthology,* Germany, 2015

'Triumvirate', *SubTerrain* Literary Journal, Vancouver, Canada, 2008

'His Golden Woman', *Women in Judaism,* Vol. 15, No. 1, University of Toronto, Canada, 2007

Acknowledgements

Dear supporters, it is you who pledged this book into existence so I will now do a little dance of thanks. My gratitude also goes to Unbound for seeing the potential of this collection and to Xander Cansell for his patient assistance. To the impressive editors: Susan Opie and Jamie Ambrose, as well as Annabel, Molly, Leonora and the incredible Unbound team. And to Mark Ecob for the inspiring cover design.

I send rays of appreciation to Alice Jolly and James Ellis for convincing me to take the leap, and to the Unbound Social Club for making the process a communal one.

Gratitude and respect goes to Joan Barfoot, my mentor at the Humber School for Writers, Toronto, who helped me bring many of these stories to their full life. To Lauren B. Davis, for reigniting my writing spark in Paris at WICE. To Dr Clare Morgan, writer, critic and Director of the MSt in Creative Writing at the University of Oxford who gave me the place and time to write, and reminded me to do so. For my peeps at The Writer's Room and in my writing group in Hamburg who supply me with the cake and enthusiasm to go on.

Heartfelt appreciation goes to Volker and to our children who arrived just on time. Last, but not least, to my parents who taught me to be curious and adventurous, my siblings for making me laugh, and to my wider circle of family and friends who continue to delight.

Patrons

Sujaritha A
Nezhla Aghaei
Kristina Agosti
Cheryl Amundsen
Fiona Beaton
James Benmore
Cherryl Bird
Brer Brett
Stefan Brüdermann
Susannah Bunce
Nitesh Chaturvedi
Mara Coward
Mike Cummins
Sarah Daunis
Liz Dawson
Mary de la Torre
Annette Deutschendorf
Serena Donahue
Esther Donahue
Mary Dwyer
Nele Giese
Lizzie Harwood
Donna Heizer
Tessa Hellbusch
Ian Hinkle
Agnetha Höfels
Justine Huang
Brigitte Hyde
Chrissy Lee Jing-Jing
Amalia Juneström
Glen Kanwit
Shona Kinsella

Janet Kinsey
Lutz Kramer
Jing-Jing Lee
Marti Leimbach
Jenny Lewis
Ian MacDonald
Paul Matthews
Catherine McNamara
Stacey Merkl
Erinna Mettler
Leslie Moore
Joana Moths-O'Neil
Carrie Anne Nolte
Jamie Nuttgens
Roanne O'Neil
Courtney Peltzer
Jennifer Pierce
Martina Plieger
Sarah Plochl
Anna Polonyi
Hartmut Pospiech
Sascha Preiß
Verena Rabe
Sadiq Rahman
Dennis Riebenstahl
Alex Robertson
Amy Rodenburg
Auriel Roe
Catherine Schwerin
Tessa Scott
Marcus Speh
Olga Szymczyk
Liz Thompson
Mike Scott Thomson
Lexi von Hoffmann
Martina Weiner

Thomas White
Shena Wilson
Kristiana